Missy Piggle-Wiggle
and the
Won't-Walk-
the-Dog Cure

Based on the Mrs. Piggle-Wiggle series of
books and characters created by Betty MacDonald
and Anne MacDonald Canham

Missy Piggle-Wiggle

and the

Won't-Walk-
the-Dog Cure

ANN M. MARTIN

with ANNIE PARNELL

illustrated by BEN HATKE

Feiwel and Friends
New York

A FEIWEL AND FRIENDS BOOK
An imprint of Macmillan Publishing Group, LLC

Our books may be purchased in bulk for promotional, educational, or business
use. Please contact your local bookseller or the Macmillan Corporate and Premium
Sales Department at (800) 221-7945 ext. 5442 or by e-mail at
MacmillanSpecialMarkets@macmillan.com.

Library of Congress Cataloging-in-Publication Data

Names: Martin, Ann M., 1955– author. | Parnell, Annie, author. | Hatke, Ben,
    illustrator.
Title: Missy Piggle-Wiggle and the Won't-Walk-the-Dog Cure / Ann M. Martin
    with Annie Parnell ; illustrated by Ben Hatke.
Description: First edition. | New York : Feiwel and Friends, 2017 | Series:
    A Missy Piggle-Wiggle book | Summary: Even though Missy Piggle-Wiggle
    is preoccupied with repairing her upside-down house that was damaged in a
    storm, she always finds time to administer her magical cures that rid children
    in Little Spring Valley of their unwanted habits and misbehavior. | Description
    based on print version record and CIP data provided by publisher; resource
    not viewed.
Identifiers: LCCN 2016045718 (print) | LCCN 2017021275 (ebook) |
    ISBN 978-1-250-07170-5 (hardcover) | ISBN 978-1-250-13519-3 (ebook)
Subjects: CYAC: Behavior—Fiction. | Magic—Fiction. | Humorous stories.
Classification: LCC PZ7.M3567585 (ebook) | LCC PZ7.M3567585 Mm 2017 (print) |
    DDC [Fic]—dc23
LC record available at https://lccn.loc.gov/2016045718

Book design by Eileen Savage

Feiwel and Friends logo designed by Filomena Tuosto

First edition, 2017

10   9   8   7   6   5   4   3   2   1

For librarians everywhere, and in memory of
Mr. Counts, who made the library come alive for
me at Littlebrook Elementary School.
—A.M.M.

~~~~~~~

For Betty, Grandma, Mom, and all the Anne
Elizabeth Campbells who came before them.
—A.P.

CONTENTS

Missy Piggle-Wiggle
and the
Won't-Walk-
the-Dog Cure

Dear Missy,

I'm afraid this is yet another letter written in haste, as I believe I'm closing in on my husband and the rest of the pirates. I'm sorry that so many months have gone by since my last letter, but you understand how important it is to me to find Mr. Piggle-Wiggle. This is just the sort of challenge one encounters when one marries a pirate, and one must take one's time and tread lightly.

I trust that all is well at the upside-down house, and I'm very, very grateful to you for taking care of things. I miss Wag; I miss Lester and Lightfoot and Penelope and the residents of the barn and farmyard. I miss the children and families of Little Spring Valley. And I miss you.

Can you stay on a bit longer? How is the money holding out? Have you needed to search for the silver key yet? If you have and you still need money, well, there are always Mr. Piggle-Wiggle's gold doubloons. But I would rather you not sell them, for reasons you well understand.

With apologies,

Your loving and grateful Auntie

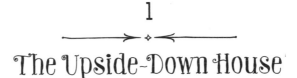

1

The Upside-Down House

IF YOU WERE to walk north along Juniper Street, which is the main street in the town of Little Spring Valley, and pass by all the shops and businesses until you came to Aunt Martha's General Store, and then turn on to the very next street on the left, you might think, *Hmm. What a nice, ordinary little town.* You would pass brightly colored houses with porches in the front, and trimmed lawns with children and dogs and pots of flowers, and bicycles and scooters lying about.

And then you would come to a house that was upside down, with its roof poking into the ground and its bottom waving toward the sky. There's a regular-looking porch on this upside-down house, with steps to the front door, because how else could you get into the house? But the chimney of the house starts at the slope of one of the upside-down roofs and tunnels into the ground. Since some of the bricks have fallen out of the chimney, it makes an especially good climbing wall with lots of helpful footholds, and the children of Little Spring Valley scamper up and down it like monkeys. The windows of the upside-down house open from the top, not the bottom, and, inside, the ceilings are the floors and the floors are the ceilings. Chandeliers sprout out of the floor like cabbages, and sometimes the chairs and couches are just where you'd want them in order to sit down, but sometimes they're hovering above your head or turned downside up.

Who lives in this house? That's a perfectly reasonable question. The house was built many years ago by a pirate named Mr. Piggle-Wiggle for his bride, Mrs. Piggle-Wiggle. When Mrs. Piggle-Wiggle was a little girl, she dreamed of one day living in an upside-down house. So her husband built her the house of her dreams. It isn't a very practical house, since one constantly has to leap over doorways and vacuum around the chandeliers, and it's hard to know whether to call the attic the attic or the basement, or the basement the basement or the attic, but the house is a lot of fun, and there isn't another one like it in Little Spring Valley.

Neither Mr. nor Mrs. Piggle-Wiggle lives in the upside-down house now. Mr. Piggle-Wiggle disappeared some years ago when he was called away by the pirates, who are always unpredictable. His wife missed him terribly, of course, so at last, when there had been no word from him in months and months, she decided to go in search of him, and she asked her great-niece, Missy, to stay in the upside-down house and take care of it and the animals.

So that's who lives in the upside-down house now. Missy Piggle-Wiggle.

~~~~~

On the first truly warm Saturday of spring, Missy sat up in her bed and stretched. "Good morning, Wag," she said to the little brown dog who was dozing at her feet.

You might think that the dog who lives in a magical upside-down house built by a pirate could talk, but you would be wrong. The only talking animal in the house is Penelope the parrot.

Wag let out a woof and a snort and went back to sleep.

Missy looked across the room at the wool hat she wore in cold weather and thought that today was the day she would switch her wool hat for her warm-weather straw hat. Then she looked at her cupboard of magical potions that could rid children of unwanted habits, and she wondered who in Little Spring Valley would need curing next. Last spring, there had almost been an epidemic of I-Never-Said-itis, but she had nipped it in the bud by giving Georgie Pepperpot a single dose of the Promise Potion.

Missy had learned everything she knew about magic and potions and cures and children from her great-aunt. Mrs. Piggle-Wiggle was renowned for her ways with children, and before she had gone off in search of her missing husband, the children in town had visited the upside-down house nearly every day to play with the magical little lady who lived there.

Mrs. Piggle-Wiggle could make any chore fun. Most children moaned and groaned at home if asked to hose down the porch or tidy up the mudroom. But Mrs. Piggle-Wiggle would cheerfully ask her visitors to "Swab the decks, mateys!" or "Make this place ship-shape!" and then she would time them on a stopwatch for good measure.

When problems at the homes in Little Spring Valley became acute and parents were at their wits' end because their offspring had become gum smackers or know-it-alls or tiny-bite takers, they would phone Mrs. Piggle-Wiggle for one of her magical cures, and she would always have the proper potion at hand. Missy, who, as a little girl, had spent happy vacations at the upside-down house, now knew almost as much about magic and cures as her great-aunt did.

~~~~~

Missy was reaching for her bathrobe when she heard a knock at her bedroom door.

"Come in," she called. The door opened, and in stepped a large pig carrying a tray with good smells wafting from it.

"Lester," said Missy, smiling. "Breakfast in bed? What's the occasion?"

Lester set the tray on Missy's bed and shrugged his hairy shoulders. He couldn't speak, but he was extremely polite, and Missy sometimes engaged his help when she needed to teach good manners to children who didn't need a magical potion but who nevertheless chewed with their mouths open or refused to use their napkins or grabbed handfuls of cookies without passing the plate around.

"Will you join me?" asked Missy.

Lester perched on the bed, crossed his hind legs, and poured himself a cup of coffee. He was the sort of pig who liked to drink four or five cups of coffee with each meal.

Missy, Lester, and the sleepy Wag enjoyed breakfast in Missy's room until Missy suddenly clapped her hands, said, "Saturday or not, there's work to be done," and jumped out of bed.

There are always plenty of chores to be done on a farm, and behind the upside-down house were a barn and a

farmyard. Beyond the farmyard was a pasture, so, as you might imagine, there were animals to be fed and exercised, stalls and hutches to be cleaned, and any number of things to keep Missy busy. The farm was a lot of work. Running it was expensive, too, and Missy's wallet was growing light, but so far she hadn't needed to search for the silver key her great-aunt had mentioned. She hadn't sold the precious gold doubloons, either. Gold is valuable and would fetch a pretty price. But gold *doubloons* are the only currency worth anything in the pirate world, and Missy had a feeling in her bones that one day her great-aunt might need them in her search for her husband. Missy dared not part with even a single one.

Missy, dressed in her straw hat and a flowing palegreen dress with wispy bits trailing off of it that sparkled when the light hit them just right, greeted Lightfoot the cat and Penelope the parrot in the kitchen downstairs.

"Good morning," she said cheerfully as she set out their food. Then she glanced at nothing in particular and added, "Good morning, House."

A window shade flicked in reply, and Missy could tell that the upside-down house was in a good mood, which was a relief since House could be temperamental.

Missy scratched Lightfoot behind her ears as the cat ate her kibble. Lightfoot arched her back under Missy's hand but didn't stop eating. She missed Mrs. Piggle-Wiggle more than Wag and the others did, and Missy wondered if any of her potions worked on animals. Then again, some problems couldn't be fixed with magic.

"All right. Farm chores," announced Missy.

"About time! About time!" screeched Penelope. "Lazybones."

Missy knew she was not a lazybones, so she didn't answer. She tromped out into the farmyard with Wag at her heels and Penelope flapping after them.

"Good morning," she said to Warren the gander.

"Good morning," she said to his wife, Evelyn Goose.

"Good morning," she said to Martha and Millard Mallard, the duck couple.

Then she called a general good morning to the turkeys in their pen and the rabbits in their hutches and the chickens scratching at the warm earth. At last, she entered the barn. In the rafters above, Pulitzer the owl was just settling in after a night of hunting. "Whoo," he called sleepily to Missy before closing his eyes.

Missy fed Trotsky the horse and Heather the cow.

She was startled when she heard Penelope, who had perched herself in a tree near the house, call, "Missy, Veronica Cupcake is here!"

Missy turned to see a small girl standing outside the barn. Veronica, who lived just down the street, was one of the youngest visitors to the upside-down house and so far had not needed to be cured of anything.

"I'm bored, so I came over," Veronica announced. "What can I do?"

"Help me clean out Trotsky's stall," Missy replied.

At home, Veronica had the unwelcome habit of squinching up her face and falling to the floor in a heap if her parents or big sister asked her to do the tiniest thing, such as pick up a sweater. But here at the upside-down house, she smiled and took the muck bucket from Missy.

Missy and Veronica had become nicely muddy by the time Tulip and Rusty Goodenough arrived. Rusty was one of the first children in Little Spring Valley that Missy had cured—of his unwelcome habit of spying on his sister and the rest of his family—for which Tulip was supremely grateful.

Missy rinsed Veronica off with a watering can and

then hurried into the kitchen, where she and Lester made a pitcher of lemonade.

"Can you believe it's warm enough for lemonade?" Missy asked.

Lester gave her the thumbs-up sign, which is hard to do when one has hooves instead of fingers, and then he carried the pitcher to the front porch.

Missy followed him with a tray of glasses. She was surprised to see that playing in the front yard now were not only Veronica, Rusty, and Tulip, but also Linden Pettigrew (whom she had cured of a full-blown case of gum smacking) and Honoriah and Petulance Freeforall, twins who wouldn't soon forget how Missy had helped them change from a know-it-all and a greedy grabber into happy, thoughtful sisters. And skipping down the street came Melody Flowers, the very first child Missy had met after moving to the upside-down house and who was new in town herself. Veronica was climbing the oak tree, Rusty and Tulip were engaged in an argument over a golf ball, and the twins and Linden were busy with shovels, digging for the pirate treasure that Mr. Piggle-Wiggle was said to have buried somewhere on the property. The yard around the upside-down house was always rather holey, which Missy didn't mind too much as long as the children eventually filled the holes with flowers or planted seedlings in them. She kept two trowels handy for this very purpose.

"Lemonade!" called Missy from the porch.

Veronica slid down the tree trunk, Rusty and Tulip abandoned the golf ball, and the twins and Linden dropped their shovels. They ran breathlessly to Missy.

What do you think was the first thing any of them said as they reached for glasses of lemonade? Was it "Thank you" or "You're so thoughtful, Missy" or "Tasty lemonade, Lester"?

No. Tulip spoke first, and she exclaimed, "Rusty took my golf ball!"

"I didn't know you played golf," Missy replied.

"Well, we don't. But I found the ball on the way over here—"

"You mean *I* found it," Rusty interrupted her.

"I saw it first!" cried Tulip.

"No, I did!"

"No, I did!"

"NO, I DID!"

Missy leveled her gaze on Rusty and Tulip. All the

children on the porch knew that look, and they set down their lemonades, wondering what would happen next.

Rusty and Tulip grew quiet.

"What a thorny problem!" screeched Penelope, bobbing up and down on Lester's head.

"And it must be solved," said Missy firmly.

Veronica burped, wiped her mouth with the back of her hand, and said, "You could saw it in half." Then she added hastily, "'Scuze me."

"What am I supposed to do with half a golf ball?" asked Tulip, and Veronica shrugged.

"I guess we could share it," said Rusty. Then he added, "But I don't really want to."

"You want it all for yourself. Is that right?" Missy asked him.

"Of course!"

"And you don't want anyone else to play with it?"

"Of course not!"

"Then you should have it."

"Hey! No fair!" yelped Tulip.

"Go ahead and play with it," Missy said to Rusty.

Rusty gave her a suspicious glance, but he set his lemonade on the tray, jumped down the porch steps, leaped over two of the holes in the yard, and claimed the ball. He didn't have a golf club, so he stood on the lawn for a while, tossing the ball up and down, up and down. Then he threw it at the oak tree, aiming for an O-shaped knot, but he missed eighteen times in a row.

The children on the porch sipped their lemonade and watched him.

Rusty tossed the ball in the air again. At last he carried it back to the porch and announced, "This is boring." He handed the ball to his sister. "Here, you can have it."

"Thanks," said Tulip halfheartedly. She was standing on the porch, the golf ball resting on her palm, when it vanished. One second it was in plain sight of everyone on the porch; the next moment there was a little crackle in the air, and the ball was gone.

Tulip gaped at her empty hand.

"Huh," said Missy. "I wonder where it could be."

"Golf ball hunt!" cried Petulance, and off ran the children to search for it.

"Very tricky," squawked Penelope.

Missy sat down on a comfy seat next to Lester. Across from her sat Melody Flowers, the only child who hadn't joined the hunt. Missy smiled at her. Melody smiled back shyly.

"I was thinking," said Missy, "that today is the perfect day for a spring picnic."

"Ooh," said Melody. "On a blanket on the ground? With sandwiches and grapes and ants? Maybe we could be circus performers on the run from thieves."

Here's the wonderful thing about Missy. Most adults would have replied, "We're on the run from thieves, and we stop to have a picnic?" But Missy replied, "Perfect! Also, we're guarding an infant princess, and we have to keep her hidden."

Melody followed Missy into the kitchen, where Lester helped them prepare food for their adventure. They baked cookies in the funny old black stove (Missy noting that they were nearly out of flour) and slapped together tomato sandwiches on the table, which was a bit difficult since earlier that morning, the table and chairs had floated to the ceiling.

"Remember to bring the parrot food!" screeched Penelope.

"You know," said Melody as she placed apples and

grapes in the picnic basket, "in Utopia, which was my old town—"

Missy refrained from saying she knew perfectly well that Utopia was the town from which Melody had moved to Little Spring Valley the previous year. Melody had started bringing up Utopia with great regularity.

"—in my old town," Melody was saying, "spring came earlier than it does here. We sometimes had picnics in February."

"Hard to believe," said Penelope and cocked her head.

Missy clapped her hands briskly. "Is everything ready?" she asked. She checked the picnic basket. "Sandwiches, fruit, carrot sticks, cookies, more lemonade, and a thermos of coffee for Lester. All we need now are plates, cups, and napkins."

Lester tugged at Missy's sleeve and held out a bag.

"Lester, you're a marvel," exclaimed Missy. "You've thought of everything. Melody, why don't you call the others?"

Missy and her guests set off through the farmyard with Wag and Lester. Penelope swooped ahead of them. "There's a good place!" she called. "There's another one."

They settled on a spot at the edge of the pasture that was neither too dusty nor too muddy, and where the grass was still short and not yet prickly. Honoriah and Petulance flapped a checked blanket in the air and let it float to the ground. Lester handed around plates and cups.

"In Utopia," said Melody as she bit into a tomato sandwich, "we once had a picnic in a field, and we picked wild strawberries, and later we made strawberry shortcake."

Missy saw Petulance and Tulip glance at each other.

"I think *this* picnic is perfect," announced Honoriah.

"It's getting a little cloudy," said Melody. "In Utopia—"

"I like clouds," Rusty interrupted her.

"Hey, Missy," said Veronica. "You should have brought your boyfriend with you."

"And just who is my boyfriend?" asked Missy.

"*You* know. Harold Spectacle." Veronica sang the name like this: "Har-old Spec-ta-cle."

Missy hoped she wasn't blushing. "He couldn't

come. The bookstore will be especially busy today. Everyone will be out shopping in this lovely weather."

"*Is* he your boyfriend?" asked Tulip.

"Stop talking about boyfriends!" exclaimed Linden Pettigrew. "I'm trying to eat."

"You know my friends Pollyanna and Ashley-Sarah? From Utopia?" said Melody.

"I'm sure they had boyfriends, even though they were eight," said Honoriah.

"Well, yes."

"Of *course*," said Petulance. She shook her head and giggled.

Missy stood up then, her dress trailing behind her in the wind that was blowing across the pasture. She shaded her eyes with her hand and stared into the distance.

"What is it?" asked Linden.

"Are the thieves after the baby princess?" exclaimed Melody.

"No," said Missy. "This is real. I think it's time to end the picnic. A storm is coming."

Lester stood up and followed Missy's gaze. He frowned. Wag woofed softly. Penelope called, "Hurry! Hurry!"

The sky to the west had turned a dark shade of purply green. Thunder rumbled. The wind lifted Missy's straw hat from her head and sent it tumbling through the pasture. Rusty ran after it, and the others tossed plates and grape stems and half-eaten cookies into the picnic basket.

"Is it a tornado?" shrieked Veronica.

"No, but it's a big storm," said Missy. "Hurry, everyone."

Missy and the children ran through the farmyard, Melody holding tight to Missy's hand. Wag and Penelope raced ahead, and Lester lumbered along behind. He wasn't a very fast pig. By the time they reached the back door of the upside-down house, rain was pelting from the sky.

"I'm soaked," said Tulip, panting, as she hurtled through the door and into the kitchen.

"Soaked!" agreed Veronica.

A flash of lightning lit the farmyard, and in the very next second, the light went out in the kitchen and the refrigerator whirred to a stop.

"Power failure," whispered Linden.

"Everybody in the basement," said Missy.

"You mean the attic?" asked Petulance.

"I thought you said this wasn't a tornado," whimpered Melody.

"I don't know what it is," replied Missy, "but the basement is a safe place during a storm."

Petulance started to run upstairs, but Missy grabbed her and said, "The attic, then. We need to be belowground."

"What about Trotsky and Heather and—" Rusty started to say.

"The animals know how to find shelter." Missy hustled Rusty and the other children into the attic-basement. Lester, Wag, Lightfoot, and Penelope hurried after them. They had barely reached the bottom step when a terrific crash of thunder sounded from above.

The upside-down house shook.

2

The Storm

MELODY COULDN'T HELP herself. She let out a long scream. "AUGHHHHHH!" She screamed so loudly that she made herself cough.

Wag ran for a corner and stood facing it, his tail between his legs, while Lightfoot climbed all the way up Missy as if she were a tree and tried to burrow under her hat. Polite Lester, who could usually be counted on to remain calm, began to snort in a way that did not sound mannerly at all but was perfectly appropriate for a frightened pig.

Penelope, for once, had absolutely nothing to say.

"Is everyone—" Missy began to ask. But at that moment, thunder crashed again.

The attic was as dark as dark can be. *As dark as a pocket*, Mrs. Piggle-Wiggle would have said.

Missy held her hands in front of her face and couldn't see them.

"Where is everyone?" asked a tiny voice.

"Veronica?" said Missy. "Is that you? Are you all right? Let's all try to hold hands."

"I'm not holding hands with any girls," announced Linden.

Girls?! thought Tulip. *What about pigs?* But fortunately she didn't say that aloud.

What followed was a lot of scrambling around and cries of "Where's Honoriah?" and "That's my nose, not my hand!" and "Let go of my hair!" and "AUGHHHHHHH!" (That was Melody again.) But at last everyone was holding hands and hoofs.

"Are we all okay?" asked Missy. She took roll call. She made sure she could feel Lightfoot on her head, Penelope on her shoulder, Wag's rump in the corner, and Lester's hoof in her left hand. Then she called out, "House? Are you okay, too?"

The house replied by opening and closing the door at the top of the stairs.

"Good," said Missy in her calmest voice. "This is a big storm, but we're all together and we're all fine. We'll just have to wait it out."

"We could pretend we're pioneers without electricity," suggested Petulance in a whisper.

"And we've been put in a dungeon," said Veronica.

"Who would put pioneers in a dungeon?" asked Rusty.

CRASH.

This time the clap of thunder was followed by a crash of a different kind. Missy heard something heavy fall above her. She heard wood splinter and glass break, and she knew that something very bad had happened.

She took roll call again. Four animals and seven children were accounted for.

"House?" said Missy. "House?" She paused. "Are you all right?"

She waited for the door to open or the stairs to creak, but there was nothing.

~~~~~

"I think the storm is letting up," said Rusty after a while. "It isn't raining so hard."

"The thunder is going away," said Melody, sounding relieved but not letting go of the hands she was holding, even though Rusty was trying to shake her loose.

Five minutes later, Missy looked up the stairs and saw a beam of light coming from the kitchen. "The electricity is back on," she said. "I think it's safe to leave the basement. But be careful."

Every single child in the basement ignored Missy's warning and went charging up the stairs like a bull. Tulip ran into Honoriah, and Linden tripped over Wag. They crowded into the kitchen and peered out the window.

"Ooh, look! Everything's all blown around," said Veronica with great excitement.

"The trash can is lying on its side," Rusty reported. "There's garbage all over the place."

"The farmyard looks like a lake," said Petulance. (That was a huge exaggeration.)

Missy picked up her phone. "Call your parents," she instructed the children. "Let them know you're okay."

"Trouble!" squawked Penelope from the front of the upside-down house. "Trouble!"

Missy hurried through the kitchen and the hallway and opened the door to the porch. She looked out into the yard, which was now dotted with holes full of muddy water. The golf ball floated in one of them.

Missy's gaze traveled to the right, and she let out a sigh.

"Oh, no," she said. "Poor House. Poor, poor House."

The very tall oak tree, the one Veronica had climbed earlier, had blown over, roots and all, and was leaning at an angle. Missy's gaze followed the trunk

up,

up,

up

to the top of the tree.

It had smashed through the upside-down house. The windows of the attic (or the basement, or the basement-attic) were shattered, and Missy saw glass glinting on the ground below. The roof and one of the third-story walls had splintered and caved in. Below, on the second floor, Mrs. Piggle-Wiggle's bedroom window was broken and another part of the wall had been smashed in.

"Poor House," Missy said again, and tutted just like her great-aunt would have done.

But then she straightened her back, told herself to buck up, and returned to the kitchen. "Make sure you keep your shoes on," she said to the children. "There's broken glass outside. I'll wait with you until your parents pick you up."

~~~~~

Half an hour later, Missy stood alone in the living room of the upside-down house. She stared at her phone for a moment and finally called Harold Spectacle, the owner of A to Z Books on Juniper Street. The Harold who might or might not be her boyfriend.

"Harold," she said, "um, I was wondering. How did you fare in the storm?" Like most people who are good at helping others, Missy was not very good at requesting help for herself. She asked Harold two questions about the store and one about his general health before she managed to say, "A tree fell through my house. Do you think you could come over?" She did not say that she was nervous and needed moral support, even though she was and she did.

Of course, Harold said he would be there as soon as he could leave the store.

"Thank you," said Missy. Then she punched in the number of Aaron's Ace Repairs, which was the first home repair company in the Little Spring Valley phone directory.

"I won't be able to come myself," said Aaron, "since, as you can imagine, the storm caused a lot of damage and everyone is calling, but I'll send someone to your house right away. Where are you located?" Missy gave him the address and he said, "I guess you won't be hard to find, what with a tree through your roof."

"Also," said Missy, "the house is upside down."

She heard raucous laughter on the other end of the line as they hung up.

Harold arrived before the repairperson did. He came running along the street in his red velvet tuxedo, one hand clapped to his top hat in order to keep it in place. Missy realized she had never seen Harold run before. In his free hand, he was carrying the cane he didn't actually need, and he brandished it like a hockey stick, shoving fallen branches and bits of trash out of his way.

"Missy!" he called as he approached the walk to the upside-down house. "Are you really all right?"

"Right as rain," she replied. "But I'm afraid House isn't up to snuff."

"Deary me." Harold picked his way along the muddy path as fast as he could. "That was quite a storm, wasn't it? Entirely unexpected. I didn't hear anything about it on the weather this morning." He stopped talking when he saw Missy's face. "You don't *look* right as rain," he said.

"I'm just a little worried about poor House. I haven't been upstairs yet." Missy didn't want to admit that she was afraid of what she might see there.

"Are the animals okay?"

"Mostly. Lightfoot is hiding under the kitchen table, Wag is hiding under my bed, and Lester is lying on the couch with a cloth over his eyes. They didn't like the thunder. Penelope is fine, though. She loves drama." Missy paused. "I called Aaron's Ace Repairs. Someone should be here soon."

Missy and Harold walked around the yard, picking up branches and broken shingles and soggy bits of paper and stuffing them in a garbage bag.

"Hey!" exclaimed Harold. "I found a golf ball."

At that moment, Missy heard a loud honk and turned to see a truck parking in the street. The lettering on the side read: AARON'S ACE REPAIRS. "Oh, good," she said. "He's here."

But the person who climbed out of the truck was a she, not a he. Every piece of her clothing was embroidered with the words AARON'S ACE REPAIRS—her cap, her overalls, the sleeve of her shirt.

"Missy!" she cried. "Is that really you?"

Missy stared at the woman. "I, um—"

"Serena Clutter. I used to see you here when we were little, remember? We played together when you were visiting your great-aunt?"

And suddenly Missy did remember Serena. She also remembered secretly testing out a potion on Serena when she was first learning magic and briefly turning Serena into an enormous pigeon, which she sincerely hoped Serena had forgotten about.

"Hello!" Missy exclaimed nervously.

"In town for a visit?" asked Serena. She opened the back of the truck and hauled out a large tool kit.

"Actually, I'm living here now. My great-aunt is away for a while."

"The pirates?"

"Yup."

Serena stood for a moment and gazed up at the house. "Wow," she said. "That's a shame."

"Do you think you can repair it?" asked Harold.

"Well . . . yes. Let me take a look around. There's quite a bit of damage."

"Uh-oh," said Missy, glancing at Harold.

"But I'm sure it can be fixed."

Missy led Serena into the upside-down house and up to the second floor. Harold followed them.

"This is my great-aunt's room," said Missy. She stood firmly in the doorway and made herself look in. She held her chin high. "Oh," she said after a moment. Glass and leaves and debris covered every surface of the room. The window and wall had crumbled over the bed.

"Deary me," muttered Harold again.

Missy looked at Serena and raised her eyebrows.

"Nothing that can't be repaired," said Serena after a moment. "But it will take some time."

"I don't want the animals going in there," said Missy. She closed the door and led Serena to the end of the hall, next to her own bedroom. "The attic is just up these stairs," she said. She reached for the doorknob, then jerked her hand back. "Ow!" she cried.

"What's the matter?" asked Serena. "Is it stuck? Here, let me try."

"No, don't!" Missy blew on her hand. The knob had felt like a lump of burning coal. She turned to the door and said soothingly, "House, Serena is here to help you. She needs to go upstairs so she can look at the rest of the damage." Then she turned back to Serena and Harold. "House is a bit upset," she whispered.

Serena nodded. "I remember House's moods."

The house rumbled, then shook the hallway like someone flapping a rug into place. Missy, Harold, and Serena lost their balance and fell on the floor in a heap.

"Hey!" exclaimed Serena.

"House doesn't like being talked about," Missy explained. Then she added in a louder voice, "But that's no excuse for this behavior, House. How is Serena going to help you if you won't let us see what needs to be fixed? Now, please—good manners."

Missy reached for the doorknob again. It was cool. "Thank you," she said. She turned the knob and led the way to the attic.

"Oh my," said Harold when he and Missy and Serena were standing at the top of the stairs.

A voice behind them screeched, "Chaos! Chaos!"

Missy ignored Penelope, who had followed them and was now perched on Harold's hat. She gazed around the attic and let out a large and very loud sigh. The attic, which was much more attic-y than basement-y (because Mr. Piggle-Wiggle had luckily realized that a third floor made of stone would have created an unfortunately top-heavy house) was a shambles. The oak tree had smashed through the roof, a window, and a large section of wall. Storage boxes and shelves and cabinets had been smashed, too, and scattered everywhere were those odd things that somehow always wind up in attics—lamps that won't light anymore, cups without saucers, coats with holes in them, and boots and books and blankets. Just then, because sometimes when you think things can't possibly get any worse, they do anyway, rain began to fall again, and it spattered through the hole and widened the puddles on the floor.

"Be careful where you step," said Harold. "I'm not sure the floorboards are going to hold up."

Missy sank down onto a damp carton. "Are you *sure* you can repair . . . this?" she said to Serena, waving her hands to indicate all that needed to be done.

Serena placed her hands on her hips. She walked to the broken window and leaned out, looking at the wall below. Then she turned around and surveyed the attic again. "I am," she said at last. "But it's going to be a big job."

"When can you start?"

"I'll have to check with Aaron, but I think we can start on Monday. I'll come back with a crew."

"Hear that, House?" said Missy.

The house responded by sending a blast of cold air through the hole in the roof. Papers and twigs coiled themselves into a cyclone.

"Pardon me for saying so, but that wasn't very helpful," said Serena, frowning, as the mess settled. "Is House going to let us make our repairs?" She was prying up boards and peering behind the plaster on the walls. Before Missy could answer her, Serena went on. "This is going to be hard enough with all the backward wiring. And upside-down windows. And upside-down doorways. And—" She paused and glanced at the ceiling. "Was that trunk floating up there before?"

"We'll make it work," Missy assured her. "I'll have a talk with House."

"In the meantime," said Serena, "I'll cover the hole with a tarp."

On Sunday, Missy sat at the dining room table with a large piece of cardboard and several fat markers. This was the same dining table at which visiting children made macaroni sculptures and Popsicle-stick boxes and learned how to knit. Missy spread newspaper over the table and set to work. She lettered a sign that read: CLOSED FOR REPAIRS.

As she worked, the table and chairs slowly rose toward the ceiling. Missy waved at Wag and Lightfoot below and then called cheerfully, "House, could you please lower me?" The table wobbled downward and settled onto the rug. Missy stood up from her chair as if she were getting off of a ride at an amusement park. She carried the sign outside and nailed it to the railings of the porch.

When she turned around, she saw Beaufort Crumpet (known for his love of all things sugary), Georgie Pepperpot, Samantha Tickle (now cured of her case of constantly needing "just one more minute"), Tulip, and Veronica standing in a mournful row on the sidewalk. They were staring at the sign.

"You can't close the upside-down house!" exclaimed Georgie.

"It's against the law," called Veronica.

"It is not against the law," replied Missy.

"It is, and I'm going to call the police."

"How long is it closed for?" asked Samantha, who was older than Veronica and much more practical.

"Until enough repairs have been made so that it's safe for you to play here again."

Veronica slumped tragically to the sidewalk and lowered her head into her lap. "That could be forever."

"The upside-down house has never been closed

before," said Beaufort, even though he wasn't sure this was true.

"Never," said Veronica from the depths of her lap.

"I'm sorry," said Missy. "What has to be, has to be."

~~~~~

On Monday morning at eight o'clock on the dot, two trucks from Aaron's Ace Repairs pulled up in front of the upside-down house. Serena and a team of workers wearing identical blue caps and overalls and shirts climbed out of the trucks.

Missy waved to them from behind the sign on the porch.

One of the workers stood on the lawn, looked at the house, and scratched her head. "Wow," she said. "Upside down."

"I told you," whispered one of the other workers.

The crew, carrying toolboxes and ladders and heavy electrical things that Missy couldn't identify, approached the porch. They looked at the upside-down door.

"Come in," said Missy gallantly, sweeping the door

open with the lower of the two knobs placed there years ago by Mr. Piggle-Wiggle.

Serena's crew entered so cautiously that Penelope, who was watching from a chandelier on the floor of the living room, called out, "Step it up!"

"Coffee?" asked Missy as Lester appeared in the hallway with a tray.

One member of the crew looked at Lester, cried, "Pig!" in the same way most people would cry "Snake!" and dropped a wrench on his foot. Then he fled up the stairs before Serena even had time to say, "It's just up those stairs."

"I think we'll have the coffee later," Missy told Lester, and he nodded and retreated to the kitchen.

It was quite a while before all the equipment had been hauled to the attic, where the repair work was to begin, and Serena had shown her crew the backward wiring and wrong-side-up windows and explained about the floor versus the ceiling.

Pierpont Demitasse, the repairman who had cried "Pig!" earlier, eyed a carton that was making its way slowly upward to a point just above his head.

"Oh, yes," Serena said. "Sometimes things float."

"But House is going to try to keep that to a minimum," added Missy loudly.

~~~~~

And so the work began. Serena and her crew were careful and respectful. They sawed up the tree and hauled away the fat trunk and all the limbs. They began fixing the roof and the wall.

The crew grew used to feeling the floor rock beneath them or finding that the doorway to the attic had shrunk to the size and shape of a mouse hole. They accepted cups of coffee from the pig. Everyone felt at home in the upside-down house except for Pierpont Demitasse, who excused himself at lunchtime on the first day of work and never came back.

On Friday afternoon of that week, Serena handed Missy a piece of paper. "This is Aaron's estimate," she said. "He thinks the work will take several more weeks."

"Okay," said Missy.

"We'll be back Monday morning, eight o'clock sharp."

Missy waved good-bye to Serena. Then she sat at the kitchen table and looked at the paper in her hands.

She gasped.

Wag came to sit at her feet, and he tipped his tail uncertainly. Lester approached, frowning. Missy handed him the estimate. Lester's eyes widened.

"I know," said Missy. "After I pay this, I'll barely have any money left. And this is just an estimate. What if the work takes longer?"

Lester pointed upstairs with one manicured hoof.

Missy nodded. "Yes. The silver key in the attic. I wish I knew what Auntie meant. Do you know anything about a silver key?"

Lester shook his head.

Missy remembered a time long ago when she was a very little girl and her great-aunt had needed money herself. There hadn't been a bit of food in the cupboards nor a penny in her pockets. But a careful search of House had revealed a great treasure left behind by Mr. Piggle-Wiggle for his beloved wife. It should have been enough to last forever, but of course very few things actually do last *forever*.

"I suppose I'll just have to be as frugal as I can for as long as I can," said Missy finally.

Penelope flapped into the kitchen. "Gold doubloons!" she squawked.

"No," murmured Missy. "Sell Uncle's doubloons?
Never."

"Never say never," Penelope croaked darkly.

3

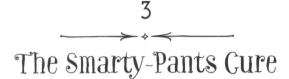

The Smarty-Pants Cure

IN AN OLD house not far from Juniper Street in Little Spring Valley lived Pandora and Marvel Treadupon and their three children. Pandora and Marvel were quiet people. They were fond of sitting on their back porch and doing absolutely nothing but listening to the birds chirping or the wind blowing. They preferred reading to talking. They held hands and smiled at each other and their children, and they enjoyed a good laugh every now and then, but they kept conversation to a minimum, and they spoke in low tones. That was just how they liked things.

For years, the Treadupon household had been so peaceful that it was the place where other parents on the street sent their children when they needed to settle down. Their next-door neighbors, the Figs, used the Treadupon home when their own children needed a time-out. One day when Mrs. Fig had asked her daughter Fedora to please clean up her bedroom, Fedora had replied, "Why don't *you* clean it up if it bothers you so much?"

Mrs. Fig, horrified, had said, "You need a time-out, young lady." Then she had looked around at the chaos in the house and said, "March next door. Right now."

Fedora Fig had headed for the Treadupons' home and sat in their silent, boring kitchen corner for ten minutes. Pandora Treadupon had waved to her from the back porch, where she was drinking tea and listening to the birds, but she hadn't said a word.

The Treadupons had three children—twelve-year-old Tallulah, ten-year-old Marvel Junior, and five-year-old Einstein. Their lives had been just as calm as calm can be until Einstein turned two. That was when he'd started speaking in complete sentences. Suddenly, the Treadupon home exploded with chatter, and it was all Einstein's. While his father was content simply to listen to the birds, Einstein would jump up and down beside him and exclaim, "Do you hear that? Do you hear that? That's a pileated woodpecker, scientific name *Hylatomus pileatus*. It inhabits deciduous forests. Do you know what *deciduous* means?" Without waiting for an answer, he would hold up his index finger and go on. "Fun fact! The holes woodpeckers make in trees become shelters for bats and birds."

While Einstein jumped up and down expounding on woodpeckers, his jacket and tie flapped about. Einstein always wore a suit. He carried a briefcase. And he insisted on being addressed by his complete formal name: Einstein J. Treadupon. He referred to his mother and sister as Ms. Treadupon and his father and brother as Mr. Treadupon.

There was nothing Einstein J. Treadupon couldn't talk about—dinosaurs, silverware, books he'd read, gum he'd found on the sidewalk.

And he was only five.

"He's a genius," Pandora would say wonderingly to Marvel Senior. "Our son is a genius. We mustn't stifle him."

"We must allow his interests to grow."

"To unfurl like petals on a flower."

Some of the Treadupons' neighbors, the Figs in particular, had a different opinion of Einstein. They didn't mind his suit and tie, but . . .

"He never stops talking!" Fedora complained to her mother.

Mrs. Fig didn't want to say so, but privately she felt that Einstein was like a windup toy that couldn't be shut off.

"And most of what he says is not at all interesting," Fedora continued. "Like when he talks about wood."

Emmy Fig, who was in Einstein's kindergarten class, said, "He never raises his hand. He interrupts Mr. Graham seven billion times a day."

Mrs. Fig shook her head. She was sorry to have lost her time-out spot in the Treadupons' kitchen, which, now that Einstein could talk, was no longer a calm oasis.

"I feel a little sorry for Pandora and Marvel," ventured Mrs. Fig over dinner that night.

"I don't," her husband replied. "What did they think was going to happen when they named their child Einstein?"

Next door, the Treadupons were also eating supper. The five of them sat at the table in their dining area.

Einstein J. Treadupon's briefcase leaned against his chair. Mr. Treadupon passed around plates of rice, broccoli rabe, and baked chicken. Back in the time before Einstein had learned to talk, Pandora, Marvel Senior, Marvel Junior, and Tallulah would have smiled at one another and spoken politely about their days. They used to have conversations like this:

MARVEL JUNIOR: Beaufort Crumpet let me feed his bunny this afternoon.

PANDORA: How lovely, dear.

MARVEL SENIOR: I've been thinking that we might go to the beach this summer.

TALLULAH: Oh, a vacation. Wonderful, Father.

Then there would have been a five- to ten-minute pause while everyone chewed their food, thought about rabbits and the beach, and listened to the classical music playing in the living room.

At last Marvel Junior might have said: Is there anything for dessert?

PANDORA: A special treat. I'll give you some money when the ice-cream truck comes around.

TALLULAH: Splendid. Thank you. I'll just start my homework while we wait for the truck.

Of course, the Treadupons could hear the ice-cream truck no matter what the season, even if their doors and windows were closed, since their house was so quiet that they could catch the sounds of things happening blocks away.

Now all that had changed. On the night of the chicken and rice and broccoli rabe, Marvel Junior politely waited for a break in a lecture Einstein was delivering on Stilton cheese, and then said in his soft voice, "Could someone please pass the broccoli rabe?"

Einstein hooted. "Wrong! Mr. Treadupon said broccoli *rab-ay*! As everyone knows, r-a-b-e is pronounced 'rob'."

"Well . . ." said Pandora, but her voice trailed off into nothingness.

"Fun fact!" her youngest child barreled on. "Broccoli rabe is a member of the *Brassicaceae* family, otherwise know as the mustard family." He reached for his briefcase, popped it open on his lap, and rustled around inside for his iPad and a sheaf of important-looking papers.

Pandora and her husband glanced at each other across the table. Their glance said as plain as day, *A genius! Our five-year-old is a genius!*

"*Regardez*," Einstein J. Treadupon continued. Occasionally he slipped into French, a language neither of his parents spoke. They didn't know how he had picked it up.

Tallulah leaned over to look at the papers. "Oh! You have information on all the—"

Einstein raised his voice a couple of notches, which is what he always did when he interrupted someone. "I'VE BEEN RESEARCHING THE GENUS (PLURAL *GENERA*)," he shouted over his sister, "and the species of families in the plant and animal kingdoms."

"Brilliant," murmured Marvel Senior.

"But Father, he interrupted me," Tallulah pointed out. "Einstein, it isn't nice—"

"YOU KNOW WHAT ELSE?" Einstein barged on. "In school today, Mr. Graham gave us a snack, and what do you think it was? *Graham* crackers! Graham crackers from Mr. Graham! And also we're going on a field trip. The kindergarten field trip is always to the firehouse." Einstein paused long enough to put a spectacularly small piece of chicken in his mouth.

"I remember my trip to the firehouse," said Marvel Junior. "Einstein, it's so cool. You get to—"

"*EXCUSEZ-MOI*, but I would like to remind everyone to refer to me by my formal and proper name, Einstein J. Treadupon."

Marvel Junior (who in truth thought his *own* name was too long and would have preferred to be called Marv) rested his chin in his hands. He found that he often wanted a nap after spending more than a few minutes with his brother.

"We have to choose partners!" cried Einstein, who had swallowed the speck of chicken. "How are we supposed to do that when there are seventeen kids in my class? Seventeen is an odd number, not to mention a prime number. Someone will have to have Mr. Graham for his partner, I guess. I hope my partner isn't Ms. Fig."

"Who's Ms. Fig?" asked Einstein's father.

"Mr. Treadupon, my goodness, you know who Ms. Fig is. She lives next door. She's in my *class*."

"You mean Emmy?" asked Tallulah.

"Who else? Ms. Fig never says a word. She's so boring. *Vraiment*, all my classmates are boring. By the way, did you know that the firehouse was built in 1920? It's going to have a big birthday soon."

Marvel Junior gazed at his little brother. "I wonder

why it is that Emmy never says anything. Have you noticed, Einstein J. Treadupon, that *no one* can say anything when you're—?"

"HEY, LOOK! Look out there!" cried Einstein, pointing out the window.

"What is it? A cardinal?" asked Pandora. "I saw a pair of cardinals this—"

"NO, I JUST WANTED to make you all look. That's a joke! Made you look! Made you look! I have a joke book here in my briefcase. I took it out of the library today. The joke book, I mean."

Pandora sighed wearily. "Darling," she began, addressing her young genius.

"The name is Einstein J. Treadupon."

"It might be polite," his mother continued, "to let—"

"*AU REVOIR!*" roared Einstein. "I must begin my homework."

"Mr. Graham gave you kindergarten homework?" asked Tallulah, frowning.

"Oh no. I gave it to myself." Einstein closed his briefcase and slid out of his chair, leaving his dinner largely untouched. His work was far more important than nourishment.

The remaining Treadupons let out sighs of relief and ate the rest of their dinner in utter silence.

〜〜〜〜

The next day, Pandora spent all morning and part of the afternoon working at her desk. She was research-ing the habits and migration patterns of hummingbirds in preparation for a long article she'd been asked to write for a scientific journal. She concentrated so long in the lovely, delicious silence that when she heard a loud voice at her elbow, she jumped and knocked over a glass of water.

"Good afternoon, Ms. Treadupon. Or perhaps I should say *bon après-midi*," said Einstein. He stood at his mother's elbow, carrying his briefcase and a black umbrella. He stared at the water dripping from the overturned glass onto the floor and added, "Did you know that water can exist in liquid, solid, *and* gaseous states?"

"Darling, do you see that you startled me? You might consider apologizing—"

"AND THAT ITS chemical formula is written H_2O, meaning that it consists of two hydrogen atoms and one oxygen atom? Also, as I have reminded you numerous times, including just last night, I would prefer to be addressed as Einstein J. Treadupon."

Pandora rubbed her temples with her fingers. She stared down at her desk, and her eyes fell upon a copy of the *Little Spring Valley Weekly News and Ledger.* Staring right back up at her, as if it were a sign, was a notice with cheerful lettering reminding readers of story time at A to Z Books that very afternoon.

Pandora's eyes widened. "Einstein J. Treadupon," she said, "I have a surprise for you. This afternoon we are going to go to story hour at the bookstore. It starts at four o'clock. Perfect timing. Your brother and sister can go with us."

"Wrong! As everyone knows, story hour is for babies," Einstein replied.

"Not according to the newspaper. It says it's for all ages. Today Mr. Spectacle is going to begin *Stuart Little.* Remember when we read *Charlotte's Web*? You had so many—"

"FUN FACT! *Stuart Little* is about a mouse, and just today I learned that baby mice are called pups."

Pandora rubbed her temples again. Four o'clock couldn't come fast enough.

~~~~~

Across town in the upside-down house, Missy Piggle-Wiggle stepped over a fat orange extension cord that snaked up the stairs to some piece of equipment Serena Clutter had brought inside and answered the ringing phone that Lester handed her. She listened for a moment, then said, "That sounds lovely, Harold. Of course I'll come. I'll see you a little before four." She clicked off the phone and smiled at Lester. "I think I might have a date. Harold just invited me to story hour at A to Z Books."

Half an hour later, Missy set off for town. She was surrounded by Melody, Veronica, the Freeforall children, and Beaufort Crumpet. They had been playing at the upside-down house, which was once again open to the children in town, but only if they stayed out of the way of Serena and her team, and they were frankly tired of dodging them. When they reached Juniper Street, the children ran ahead of Missy and crowded into the store. Missy followed more sedately. She stopped outside the window and, while pretending to look at a display of picture books about April showers and May flowers, adjusted her straw hat and patted her wild red hair into place. Then she entered A to Z Books. The door, which sneezed rather than ding-donged when it was opened, announced her arrival with an alarmingly realistic *AH-AH-AH-CHOO!*

"Missy, you're here," said Harold warmly, clasping her hand between both of his. "Please have a seat," he added gallantly.

Missy glanced at the row of chairs that had been arranged along the back wall for the adults. Then she plopped down onto the floor with the children. She looked around the crowded store. In addition to Veronica, Melody, Beaufort, and the Freeforalls, she saw Rusty and Tulip, Linden Pettigrew, Samantha Tickle, and Della and Peony LaCarte, sisters who most adults in town thought to be absolutely perfect. The door sneezed again, and in walked a very tired-looking mother followed by a girl of about twelve, a younger boy, and then a very small boy who was dressed in a suit and carrying a briefcase and an umbrella.

Samantha Tickle let out a groan.

"What's wrong?" Missy asked her.

Samantha turned desperate eyes on Missy. "See that boy with the briefcase? That's Einstein J. Treadupon. He's a smarty-pants. He never lets anyone say anything because he talks all the time. He's not interested in what other people have to say. Which is SO RUDE."

"That tiny little boy?"

"Yes."

"He isn't talking now. He's reading something in his briefcase."

"Well, just wait," said Samantha. Then she put her hand to her forehead and added, "The entire day is ruined."

Missy looked for the rest of the Treadupon family and saw that they had seated themselves as far as possible from Einstein. She noticed an empty chair next to Mrs. Treadupon and decided to sit there instead of on the floor. She and Einstein's mother had just exchanged smiles when Harold stood up and addressed the audience.

"Thank you all for coming today," he said. "I see

some familiar faces and some new faces. Today we'll begin reading *Stuart Little*, by—"

"It's by E. B. White!" announced Einstein. He snapped his briefcase shut. "E. B. White also wrote *Charlotte's Web* and *The Trumpet of the Swan*. AND he wrote for adults. He was a crossover—"

Harold plastered a smile on his face. He tried to talk over Einstein. "Thank you," he interrupted him. "*Stuart Little* is a book that appeals to all ages, so it's a perfect choice for our story hour. I'm happy to see plenty of adults here today as well as young people. The last book we read was—"

"THE LAST BOOK WE READ in my class at school was a picture book," said Einstein, "and in my opinion, it would have been appropriate for a much younger audience."

"Wonderful, wonderful," murmured Harold. He leaned his cane in a corner and sat on a chair at the front of the crowd. A tiny girl reached out to touch one of his polished purple shoes, and Harold smiled at her. He opened *Stuart Little*, glanced nervously at Einstein, and began reading. He had read for approximately one minute when Einstein jumped to his feet and said, "In case anyone is confused, the reason it says in the story that first-class mail is only three cents is because the book was published in 1945."

The small girl who had stroked Harold's shoe began to cry. "Why did you stop reading?" she wailed.

Missy looked at Mrs. Treadupon and saw that she was pretending to search busily through her purse. She looked at Harold and saw that he was looking at Mrs. Treadupon, too. Mrs. Treadupon kept up her desperate search. At last Harold said, trying not to focus directly on Einstein, "I would just like to remind everyone that it would be polite to hold all comments until I've finished reading today. Or at least until the end of a chapter. There will be plenty of time for discussion later."

As you might imagine, story time with Einstein in the audience was neither entertaining nor relaxing. He jumped up and down, referred to papers in his briefcase, and announced many facts that were fun only for him. One time he leaped up to exclaim, "Did you know that a pound of feathers weighs exactly the same as a pound of pennies? It's just that you need a lot more feathers than pennies to make up a pound."

"Excuse me," said Rusty, "but in case you didn't

notice, Harold was right in the middle of the best part of the story."

"Wrong! The best part of the story is when Stuart goes down the bathtub drain on the string."

"Einstein," said Harold, "if you could please refrain from interrupting, that would—"

"The name is Einstein J. Treadupon!"

"As I said, please no more interrupting."

Missy thought she detected an unusual note of exasperation in Harold's voice. Once again she glanced at Mrs. Treadupon. This time she saw that Einstein's mother was rubbing her forehead and frowning.

Missy touched her arm and whispered, "Is that your little boy?" She nodded toward Einstein.

"Yes. I'm so sorry. I do apologize."

"He's quite brilliant," said Missy.

"A genius."

"I imagine he's hard to keep up with. He seems . . ." Missy trailed off, trying to find a nice way to say that Mrs. Treadupon's son was a smarty-pants of the worst kind.

Before she could come up with something that wasn't insulting, Mrs. Treadupon looked closely at her

and whispered, "Oh, I beg your pardon. You're Missy Piggle-Wiggle, aren't you? Mrs. Piggle-Wiggle's great-niece? I heard you'd moved here. You're living in the upside-down house?"

"Yes." Missy smiled at her.

"I'm Pandora Treadupon. Einstein J. Tread—I mean, Einstein is my youngest child." She hesitated then whispered, "I've also heard that you have cures for children. Is that true?"

"Absolutely. Are you wondering if I might have a cure for Einstein?"

Pandora looked greatly relieved. She let out her breath. "Yes. Do you?"

"Right here in my purse," said Missy, patting her handbag. Smarty-pantsiness was so common and so disruptive that Missy carried the cure around with her. It was incredibly helpful in emergencies such as this.

Pandora suddenly appeared nervous. "What exactly is the cure? Einstein is terribly smart, but he's never learned to swallow pills."

"Oh, the cure isn't a pill."

"He isn't very cooperative about swallowing medicine, either."

Missy rustled around in her handbag and withdrew a small green vial. It looked like a teeny, tiny bottle of ginger ale. "All I have to do is uncork this," she whispered.

"That's it?"

"That's it. The rest will unfold on its own."

Missy worked the cork out of the mouth of the bottle. Pandora watched in fascination as a bit of blue mist trailed upward, then picked up speed and made a beeline for Einstein. It settled around his head before vanishing.

Pandora craned her neck and peered at her son. "Really," she said, "I don't quite see how that's going to accomplish anything."

"Just wait."

Mrs. Treadupon continued to stare at her son. He seemed occupied by a particular piece of paper in his briefcase.

In the front of the room, Harold came to the final sentence of the first chapter, read it, and said, "And that's the end of chapter one."

"Do you have to stop reading?" asked the girl at his feet, her voice quavering.

"Nope. We'll go right on to the second chapter, which is called—"

Einstein suddenly came to life. He slammed the briefcase closed and shot to his feet. "'Home Problems'!" he proclaimed. "It's called 'Home Problems'!"

"Oh, dear," murmured Pandora.

"Patience," whispered Missy.

"In my opinion, however," Einstein continued, "what the chapter should be called . . ." He hesitated. "What it should be called," he said again, and trailed off. He was finding it very difficult to speak. His voice was screeching and scratching like bicycle tires coming to a fast stop on a gravel road. "What it should be," he croaked, and then he came to a complete stop. He put his hands to his throat.

Pandora started to get to her feet. "He's choking!" she said.

"No, he's fine," Missy replied.

Einstein opened and closed his mouth several times. No sound came out.

"He looks like a salmon," commented Tulip.

"Wait, now I can speak," said Einstein suddenly. (Missy heard groans from all the adults and all the children.) "What I was going to say is that chickens cart around buckets from the ocean."

Everyone stared at him.

Finally his brother said, "What?"

Einstein was frowning. "I said plain as day that the environment is riddled with snakes and telephones."

Frankfort Freeforall, who was sitting next to Einstein, began to laugh and laughed so hard that he fell over on his side.

"Fun fact!" Einstein tried again, holding up his finger. "Cabinetry, I mean sophistry, I mean to say that time is getting away from all the rugs."

"Goodness," murmured Pandora.

Einstein coughed. Then, undaunted, he grabbed a pad of paper and a pencil from his briefcase. He began to write something, but Harold was reading again, and everyone became riveted to the story. No one paid any attention to the paper Einstein flashed around.

For a brief period of time, the only sound in the room was Harold's voice. Then Einstein suddenly said, "Mice are . . . Miiiiiiice . . . aaaaaaare." His voice screeched and squawked and faded away. His mouth flapped open and shut. He sighed then straightened his tie and smoothed out his gabardine suit pants.

The chapters in *Stuart Little* are not very long, so Harold read four of them before he gently closed the book and rested it on his lap. He glanced nervously down at the little girl by his feet, but she had fallen asleep. "I think this is a good stopping place," said Harold quietly. He hesitated then went on. "*Now* is the time for questions and comments. Who has something to say about what I just read?"

Six children and one of the adults raised their hands.

Harold pointed to Melody. "Yes?"

"This is one of my favorite books," said Melody shyly. "I've read it before, and each time—"

"I'VE READ IT, TOO!" cried Einstein. "The thing about reading any book more than once is that bunk beds are their fattest when the scanner isn't working."

Veronica Cupcake looked solemnly at Einstein. "You're not making any sense. Do you need a nap?"

"I'm not tired," Einstein replied crabbily. "I'm perfectly responsive to jelly rolls and what they mean."

"See? See?" exclaimed Veronica. "He's not making

any sense, is he, Melody? Is he?" Veronica looked at Melody and then at the room in general.

"Why don't you finish what you were going to say?" Harold suggested to Melody.

"Well, I was going to say that before I moved here, when I lived in the town of Utopia—"

"YOU KNOW," said Einstein, "the term *utopia* is basically a foundation for pond water and flagpoles." He leaned over to Frankfort and whispered, "Mr. Freeforall, did I just say 'pond water and flagpoles'?"

"Yup."

"Hmm."

"If we could please have some discussion about *Stuart Little*," said Harold, "that would be . . . refreshing. Melody?"

"I was just going to say that each time I read it, I feel like I've visited an old friend."

"That's lovely, Melody," said Harold.

For several minutes, the children discussed the Little family and the fact that poor Stuart had gotten rolled up in a window shade and no one knew where he was. Finally Harold got to his feet. "Well, if there are no other comments, please join me at the back of the store for refreshments."

Einstein hesitatingly raised his hand.

Harold sucked in his breath, but merely said, "Yes, Einstein? And thank you for raising your hand."

"I think," Einstein began slowly, "I think that it was very clever of Snowbell the cat to trick the Littles, even though what he did wasn't nice." He lowered his voice. "How did that sound, Mr. Freeforall?" he asked Frankfort.

"Normal."

Einstein let out a sigh of relief.

〰〰

In the car on the way home from A to Z Books, Marvel Treadupon Jr. had an idea. He stretched his legs out, crossed his ankles, crossed his arms, appeared to be thinking deeply, and finally said, "In school today, we learned that the planet Mercury—"

"FUN FACT!" trumpeted Einstein, sitting forward in the seat.

Marvel swiveled his head to observe his brother. He was hoping to see him turn into a salmon again. He wasn't disappointed. Einstein's voice took on the screeching quality, faltered, and finally disappeared altogether.

Marvel hooted with laughter, slapping his hand on the seat. "Einstein is gulping like a fish!"

"Goodness," said Pandora.

"My name is Einstein J. Beagle!" Einstein said, finding his voice. "And picture mints are definitely scarring to the eyebrows."

Marvel hooted more loudly. "Einstein J. *Beagle!*"

Pandora looked at her older son in the rearview mirror. "Dear, what were you going to tell us about Mercury?"

"I was going to say that Mercury doesn't have any moons, and the only other planet that doesn't have any moons is . . ." Marvel glanced sideways at his brother, but Einstein sat patiently. "The only other one is Venus," Marvel finished at last. He had hoped to hear Einstein J. Beagle talk about pond water and bunk beds again.

Instead Einstein asked, "What about Pluto?"

"What *about* Pluto?"

"Well, it's considered a dwarf planet, not a regular one, so I didn't know if you were studying it."

"We are studying it," said Marvel, "and it does have moons."

"Interesting," replied Einstein.

～～～～

Later that afternoon, Tallulah said, "Mother, Father, do you think we could have hors d'oeuvres before dinner this evening? We could pretend we're having a fancy party."

"What a lovely idea," replied Pandora, and she and Marvel Senior set about preparing a tray of vegetable sticks and teeny, tiny hot dogs with toothpicks in them.

When everything was ready, Pandora said, "Let's sit down. We'll have the hors d'oeuvres in the living room."

"*Très bien, Maman,*" replied Einstein.

Tallulah, who had put on her fanciest dress and a small amount of lipstick in honor of the hors d'oeuvres, leaned forward to take a hot dog and said, "In math class today, Benedict told us that the most interesting prime number is two."

"Wrong!" roared Einstein. He bit the end off a carrot stick. "Everyone knows it's seventy-three."

Pandora studied her son. When he didn't elaborate on his answer, she said to Marvel Senior, "I got an e-mail today about a lecture on hummingbirds. It's going to be held next Saturday."

"SATURDAY," Einstein yelled, "IS NAMED FOR THE PLANET SATURN, and Saturn has sixty-two moons, which . . ."

Tallulah and Marvel Junior nudged each other as their brother's voice croaked to a stop and he said, "The cabbages from Portland . . . I mean, um . . . *La voilà le chien qui parle et le voisin du . . .*"

Mr. Treadupon turned to his wife in alarm, but she rested a reassuring hand on his shoulder. "Tallulah, dear," she said, "tell everyone your news about glee club."

Tallulah dabbed at her lipstick with a cocktail napkin. "We're going to have one more performance before school is over."

In the silence that followed, Einstein asked timidly, "When will it take place?"

"In two weeks. We're putting on a show at night, and we're charging admission, and all the money will be donated to the firehouse. The *firehouse*," she said, looking at Einstein. "The one your class will be visiting."

"Well, that's very nice of you," Einstein replied. "I'll be sure to mention it to Mr. Graham."

~~~~~

Einstein didn't interrupt anyone else during dinner that evening. After the children were in bed, Marvel Senior turned wonderingly to his wife and said, "What on earth has come over Einstein?"

Pandora thought about telling him of the adventure at the bookstore, but she found that she was all talked out. "Maybe he's growing up," she replied simply.

"Well, it certainly is a pleasant change."

Upstairs, Einstein lay in his bed, his hands behind his head, and thought about all he had learned that night. He thought about his sister's concert and a project that Marvel Junior would soon be entering in the school science fair.

Just before he had closed his door, he'd called, "Good night, Ms. Treadupon, Mr. Treadupon!"

"Good night," his sister and brother had replied. Tallulah had added, "It was nice talking to you."

It had been nice, Einstein thought. He had never realized that his brother liked science as much as

Einstein himself did, and he had learned that Tallulah was the lead alto in the glee club, but that she was more interested in raising money for the firehouse than in perfecting her solo. Furthermore, he had accumulated some extremely interesting facts that afternoon, just by listening when other people spoke.

~~~~~~

Early the next morning, the phone rang in the Treadupon house. Pandora, who had been enjoying a nice peaceful cup of tea, answered it.

"Mrs. Treadupon?" said the voice on the other end. "This is Missy Piggle-Wiggle. I was just wondering how things were going. Do you think you'll need another dose of the cure for Einstein?"

"I don't believe I will," Pandora replied. "Thank you so much, Missy. You're a miracle worker."

4

The Art of Magic

ON A BRIGHT morning with a warm breeze in the air and the early sun making dewdrops sparkle on the daffodils and tulips, Missy bustled around the yard doing her farm chores.

"Good morning, Warren and Evelyn," she said to the geese. "Your babies are lovely."

The goslings followed their parents around the yard in a little pack, endlessly peeping. *Peeppeeppeeppeep peeppeeppeeppeeppeeppeeppeep.*

"Noisy! Very noisy!" squawked Penelope in a voice that was much louder than any noise the goslings made.

Missy scooped corn for the geese out of a bin in the barn. There wasn't much left.

"What *am* I going to do?" Missy asked aloud. "I'm running out of everything. Especially money."

She turned around and studied the house. Serena and her crew had been tromping in and out, in and out, for days, leaving muddy footprints and cardboard coffee containers behind. Missy thought that if anything, the holes they were repairing looked larger, not smaller. Serena said that where repair work was involved, things often got worse before they got better.

"Things often get more expensive, too!" Penelope had squawked in reply.

Missy scattered the corn in the farmyard and then sat down on a bench to think. Wag jumped up next to her and rested his head in her lap.

"Perfect," said Missy. "I need someone to talk to." Wag raised his eyebrows, listening. "I've been wondering if I should look for work," Missy went on. "After all, before I moved to Little Spring Valley, I had a job."

Missy's job had been at the Magic Institute for Children. She'd taught magic to children lucky enough to have been accepted as students at the institute, which is located in a secret village on a secret mountain, and it's all so secret that even the students don't know exactly where they are. Missy had taught three classes: *Potions and Spells for Beginners*, *Animals— What's on Their Minds?*, and *Advanced Trickery*. One afternoon a week, she had also taught a sewing class: *Make Your Own Capes and Hats!* She had been one of the most popular teachers at the institute, especially among the younger students. And her salary had been quite good.

But Mrs. Piggle-Wiggle had needed her great-niece's help, and Missy wouldn't have dreamed of letting her down.

"Well, well, well," she said to Wag.

A voice behind her said, "You know what my father says any time someone says 'Well, well, well'?"

Missy jumped and turned around. Wag let out a startled woof.

"Sorry," said Melody Flowers. "I didn't mean to scare you."

Missy smiled at her, and Melody squeezed herself between Missy and Wag on the bench. "I just came over for a visit. Anyway," Melody went on, "my father says, 'Well, well, well. Now, that's a deep subject!'"

Missy laughed. "You're up early."

Melody nodded seriously. "Yes. Back in Utopia, I was always up with the birds. That's something else my father says. 'Up with the birds.'"

Missy got to her feet. "Well, would you like to help me clean out the stalls?"

Melody, who had cleaned out the stalls before, very much liked aiming a hose around, shooting water every which way with Missy, and pretending they were firefighters, but she said, "Oh. You have to clean the stalls this morning? I was hoping we could go into town."

"To Juniper Street? Why?" asked Missy.

"Not exactly to Juniper Street. To Spell Street."

"Ah," said Missy. "I expect the Art of Magic has opened its doors for the season. Is that it?"

"Yes! How did you know that's where I wanted to go?"

Missy tapped her head. "Just a hunch."

"Well, can you come with me?"

"I thought you were afraid of the store. I thought

you said it was dark and dreary and the store clerk spoke—"

"Magic!" Melody exclaimed, reminding Missy of Einstein J. Treadupon. "He spoke magic. He *did!*" she cried, as if Missy had contradicted her. "At least I think he did. And there was that spooky black cat in a basket, and his name was Mephistopheles."

"So why do you want to go there?"

Melody twisted her hands together. "I just do. I, um, want to show it to you."

Missy could spot a lie a mile away. She knew Melody was afraid to go to the store by herself and wanted Missy for company. What she couldn't figure out was *why* Melody wanted to go back to the Art of Magic in the first place. But Missy was patient and had a way with knotty problems, so she simply said, "Well, then, let's walk to town." She led Wag into the house, called, "Lester, you're in charge," and took Melody by the hand. They set off for Spell Street.

～～～

Missy and Melody walked first to Juniper Street, turned right, and passed Aunt Martha's General Store and

Bean's Coffee Shop. Then they passed A to Z Books and waved through the window to Harold, who was working behind the counter.

A moment later, Missy said, "Here we are. Spell Street. Ready?"

Melody shivered. "Ready."

The stores on Spell Street were all nice regular ones with their doorways at the level of the sidewalk. Except for the magic store. A sign showing a black top hat and a red wand over the words THE ART OF MAGIC swayed above a railing next to a flight of damp cement stairs leading into darkness.

"It's down there," Melody whispered, pointing. "Don't you think that's strange? And spooky? The store is belowground. That makes it harder to escape."

"Escape from what?" asked Missy.

Melody drew in a deep breath. "Let's just go." She stepped aside so she could follow Missy.

The door to the Art of Magic creaked when Missy opened it. *Creeeeee.* A hollow voice said, "Welcome to your doom."

"Your doom!" yelped Melody, and she froze on the stairs.

"It's not a real voice," Missy told her. "It's like Harold's sneezing door." She took Melody's hand again, and they stepped inside. When Missy's eyes adjusted to the dark, the first thing she was aware of was dust. "Goodness," she whispered, "somebody needs a vacuum cleaner." Everywhere she looked, she saw dust and cobwebs. Floating in the light that filtered in from two small windows above their heads were dust motes, and swirling around their feet were dust bunnies. A lean black cat pounced on one and batted it under a display case.

"Is that Mephistopheles?" asked Missy. The cat was lying on his side, kicking his hind feet as he used his front feet to feel around under the shelf. He was purring loudly, and he looked joyous.

Melody leaned away from Missy long enough to scan the store. "No," she replied. "Mephistopheles is over there in his basket, just like last time. See?"

It was on the tip of Missy's tongue to say, "That decrepit old thing?" but she didn't want to hurt the cat's feelings. At last she said to Melody, "Mephistopheles is the cat you're afraid of?"

Melody crept closer to the basket. The sleeping cat

was thin and old, curled into a tiny ball. "Well . . . I guess I didn't get a very good look at him before."

A door slammed at the back of the store, and a tall figure dressed in bright-blue robes and a pointy wizard's hat glided behind the counter. "Mwa-ha-ha!" He set down a cup of coffee. Then he lit a candle that cast flickering shadows on the walls.

Melody gasped and ducked behind Missy without letting go of her hand. "He's a real wizard," she whispered loudly.

"Melody," said Missy, "do you really think that real wizards go shopping at Bean's Coffee?"

"I don't know. He's the only wizard I've ever met."

"For heaven's sake. He's just wearing a costume. He's even pinned a name tag to his robes."

"What does the name tag say?"

"Art Magic."

Melody straightened up. "Oh. Like the name of the store."

"Can I help you?" Art Magic asked.

"We need to look around first," mumbled Melody.

Art regarded Missy. "I haven't seen you in here before." He reached for his coffee and knocked the

cup over. "Drat," he muttered as coffee ran across the counter and dripped down to the floor. The scent of hazelnut reached Missy's nose.

"Is he casting a spell? Is *drat* a spell word?" Melody asked frantically.

"It is not," replied Missy.

"Fumbles and fleas!" said Art from the floor behind the counter. "All over my shoes. Now, let me see. Where are the paper towels?" He straightened up, and his hat slid off the back of his head and landed in the coffee. "Rats and rubbish!" he exclaimed.

"Let's look around a bit," said Missy, who personally felt that someone as clumsy as Art should perhaps not have a lighted candle in his store. She and Melody wandered between the shelves, while behind them they heard bangs and small crashes and cries of "Marbles and mushrooms!" and "Bat wings and barnacles!" and "Worms and wormholes!"

"All I see," said Melody after a while, "are costumes and magic tricks." She let go of Missy's hand.

"Exactly," said Missy.

"Do you think there's anything truly magical here?"

"I think this is where someone would come if she

wanted to put on a magic show. If she needed new tricks and maybe a wand."

"A *real* magic wand?" asked Melody.

"What do you mean?"

"A wand that could do *real* magic. Like you do."

"What do you think?"

Melody shrugged.

Missy looked across the store at the counter. Art was there, making notes on a pad of paper. He dropped his pen. "Crab apples and crayfish!" He retrieved the pen then stepped around in front of the counter. "What are you looking for?" he asked pleasantly.

"Well—" Missy started to say.

"A magic kit for the little girl?"

"I'm not little!" said Melody in a voice much louder than she normally used.

Art bent over to select a box from a shelf, and his hat fell off again. He stooped to pick it up, and four pens slid out of the pocket of his robe. He sighed and set the pens and the hat on a shelf. "This is my top-of-the-line beginner's magic kit," he said, holding the box out to Missy. "Perfect for the child in your life."

"I don't think we're interested in a magic kit," Missy

replied, although she still had not one single idea what Melody *was* interested in. "Thank you, though." Art Magic looked so disappointed that Missy added, "What lovely cats you have." Most adults, she had found, could be nicely sidetracked if you brought up the subject of their children. If they didn't have any children, you could mention their pets.

Art brightened. "Mephistopheles and Snowman," he said proudly.

Melody looked at the black cat that had been chasing dust bunnies and was now sitting up straight and tall, his eyes fixed on the burning candle. She frowned. "That black kitty is named Snowman?"

"Yup." Art put his wizard hat back on and knocked the pens off the shelf. "Troubadours and trampolines!"

"Melody?" said Missy. "Are you ready to go?" She paused. "What's the matter?"

Melody was standing by a rack of black robes. Her face was frozen, and she looked as if her feet had been glued to the floor. She pointed to Snowman. "Did you see that?" she whispered to Missy.

"See what?" Missy felt as though she should whisper, too.

"Snowman just stared and stared at the candle until it went out."

Missy looked at Art's candle. The flame had indeed been extinguished. "It must have gone out by itself," she said. "There was probably a little breeze from Art's robes." But she looked from Snowman to the candle and back again.

The door to the shop opened then, and the hollow voice intoned, "Welcome to your doom."

"Hi, Art!" a young man called cheerfully as he stepped inside.

"Welcome, Patrick," Art replied. "Looking for anything in particular?"

"A deck of cards and a folding wand."

"Come with me," said Art, and led Patrick to a display near the counter.

"Missy!" cried Melody. "Did you see *that*?"

"No. What?"

Melody's mouth was gawping open and closed like Einstein's had when he couldn't speak. She gulped in some air. Finally she said in a hysterical whisper, "Snowman just made a mouse fly across the room!"

She stood in front of Missy, huffing and puffing with excitement. "A *live* mouse!"

Now, if Melody had said such a thing to her mother, her mother would have replied, "I think you're overly tired, dear." If she had said such a thing to her father, he would have replied, "Impossible. What have you been watching on TV lately?"

But Missy Piggle-Wiggle was not like most adults. She replied, "Tell me exactly what you saw."

"I saw," Melody began, and paused to huff a few more times. "I saw, well, first I noticed a mouse." *Huff, puff.* "It ran out from under that shelf over there." *Huff.* "Then I saw Snowman crouched right here by my feet." She let out one final, small puff. *Puff.* "Snowman was staring at the mouse just the way he stared at the candle."

"Mm-hmm," said Missy. What she was thinking was that of course Snowman was staring. He was a cat looking at a mouse. But she let Melody finish her story.

"And the next thing I knew, that mousie was sailing through the air! He went all the way across the store to the window." Melody pointed above her head.

Missy glanced over her shoulder to see if Art Magic was listening to Melody, but he was demonstrating a trick wand to Patrick.

"Missy, mice do not ordinarily fly," Melody said urgently.

"No, they do not."

"Do you believe me?"

"I do."

Missy turned her attention to Snowman. She looked at him intently.

"Can you read his mind?" Melody asked Missy. "What's he thinking?"

"He's thinking that Snowman is a ridiculous name for a black cat."

Melody laughed. But Missy was frowning. There was something unusual about Snowman. He reminded her of a cat who had lived at the Magic Institute for Children. The cat's name was Enigma, and just like Snowman, he could sit placidly on the floor or in his bed while he made silverware jump or hats fly off of heads.

Missy looked at Art Magic and his hat, the hat he couldn't quite control. Then she looked at Snowman.

She thought he might be laughing. "Clever boy," she whispered to him. "I know what you're up to." She turned to Melody. "Ready to go?"

"Almost." Melody walked to the back of the store and stood patiently at the counter while Art rang up Patrick's cards and trick wand.

"Well, now," Art said to her as Patrick tucked the bag under his arm and turned to leave. "Have you decided on a magic kit?"

Melody shook her head. "No. Thank you. I don't want to learn tricks. I want to learn real magic."

"Real magic?" Art repeated.

"Real magic."

Art's face reddened slightly. "What is it you'd like to be able to do? Pull an egg out of an empty hat? That would surprise your friends. Pour milk out of an empty pitcher?"

Veronica Cupcake would have stomped her foot and shouted, "NO! I *said* I wanted to learn *real* magic!" But Melody was far too polite to do such a thing. "No," she said again. "Those are just tricks."

Art's face was growing redder. "Popcorn and pandemonium," he murmured.

"What I would like," Melody said in her most grown-up voice, "is to make my dog talk, make my teeth brush themselves, turn Little Spring Valley into Utopia, that sort of thing."

"Mm-hmm, mm-hmm," said Art.

"So can you help me?" Melody asked patiently.

Art looked desperately around his store. "The most advanced kit I have," he said finally, "is the Conjure-Master 3000. It's state-of-the-art."

Melody dropped her head. "Oh. Okay. Thanks. That isn't quite . . . Let's go, Missy."

Missy reached for Melody's hand. She locked eyes briefly with Snowman, who stared at her until she felt her face turn warm. Then she and Melody climbed the steps and emerged into the sunshine.

They walked back to Juniper Street in silence. At last Melody said, "Mr. Magic doesn't know how to do real magic, does he?"

"He creates illusions," Missy told her. "He's a very good actor. And salesperson."

"Snowman might be magic."

"There's certainly something unusual about him."

Melody let out a sigh. "I guess I'll just have to ask you, then."

"Ask me what?"

"How to do real magic. I wanted to learn by myself, but Mr. Magic only has tricks. Can you teach me?"

"Teach you how to do magic?"

"Yes." Melody nodded her head once, with great finality.

"And why do you want to learn magic?"

"It's the only way to solve my problems."

"I see," murmured Missy.

"*You* solve people's problems with magic."

"Sometimes. But sometimes magic isn't the best way to solve a problem."

"It's the fastest, though, isn't it?"

"Sometimes," Missy said again.

Melody waited for Missy to ask her about her problems. When she didn't, Melody finally said, "All my friends hate me. They're not like my friends in Utopia. I've been trying and trying to make them like me, but nothing is working."

"So you thought you'd try magic."

Melody nodded again. "It must be the only way. And I *know* there's real magic because you're magic, and House is magic, and Snowman is magic. So I just need to learn some real magic."

"I'll have to think about this," said Missy, and she was glad that no one knew about her work at the Magic Institute for Children.

5

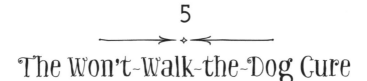

The Won't-Walk-the-Dog Cure

FLORENCE AND PERRY Dolittle thought that their lives in Little Spring Valley were nearly perfect. They lived on a pleasant street and had pleasant jobs and two very nice children, Egmont and Caramel. The children were pleasant as well, except for those times when Egmont, who was eight, would ask if he could get a pet. He never asked just once. Instead, his conversations with his parents went like this:

"Can I get a pet?"

"No."

"Can I get a pet?"

"No."

"Can I get a pet?"

"No."

"Can I get a pet?"

"No."

"Can I get a pet?"

"No."

One night, after Egmont had asked twenty-two times in a row if he could get a pet, Florence threw her hands in the air and declared to her husband, "He's relentless!" Most likely, she meant that Egmont was annoying, but she didn't want to say that out loud about her own son. It seemed wrong. Still, Egmont's quest for a pet left Florence and Perry feeling exhausted.

It was unfortunate for the Dolittles that right next door to them lived the LaCarte family. There were two LaCarte children—Della and Peony—and they were close in age to Egmont and Caramel. Everyone in Little Spring Valley knew that the LaCarte girls were perfect. They never did anything wrong. They were polite. They were on time. They didn't make messes. They cleaned up other people's messes unasked. They came directly home from school each afternoon—as sparkling clean as when they had left in the morning—and started their homework the moment they had politely thanked their mother for their healthy snack. They helped each other with their homework. They didn't fight over what to watch on TV, because they had long ago agreed that watching TV was not a productive use of their time.

The reason it was unfortunate for the Dolittles that the LaCartes were their neighbors was because Florence and Perry knew with absolute certainty that if Della and Peony had asked for a pet, the conversation would have gone like this:

"Could we please get a pet?"

"I'm afraid not."

"Okay. Thank you for considering our request."

The Dolittles couldn't figure out where they had gone wrong.

"It must be our fault," Perry said to his wife the night Egmont asked for a pet twenty-two times.

"What must be our fault?"

Perry shook his head. Suddenly he wasn't sure. "All I know is that the LaCartes have never had this problem."

"The LaCartes have never had any problem with their angels."

Caramel, who was seven, had been listening at the door to her parents' bedroom. "I think Della and Peony come from outer space," she announced. She hurtled herself into the room and flopped onto the bed. Then she said, "Anyway, couldn't you just *talk* to Egmont about getting a pet? Maybe all he wants is a teensy little goldfish or something."

Florence and Perry looked at each other in surprise. "Carrie, how perceptive of you," said her mother.

"Why, of course," added Perry. "We must have a conversation with Egmont instead of cutting him off every time he brings up the subject."

Mr. and Mrs. Dolittle felt quite pleased about this turn of events. "I was beginning to think we might need to ask Missy Piggle-Wiggle for advice, but instead we've solved the problem all by ourselves!" said Florence.

"And simply by listening to our daughter," said Perry. Secretly, he was thinking, *This must be the sort of thing that goes on all the time next door.*

It's important to know that Egmont was a very nice boy when he wasn't asking over and over if he could get a pet. He wasn't perfect like Peony and Della, but then, nobody was, except Peony and Della themselves.

Egmont was known in school for his imagination. He kept notebooks full of stories and poems with titles like "The Perfect Horse for Me," "Guinea Pigs I Have Known," and "How the Peacock Got His Tail." Once, he won fifty dollars in a newspaper contest for young writers with his story called "Oink! Oink! Meow!" about a pig who wanted a kitten. He donated the prize money to Friends Furrever, Little Spring Valley's animal shelter, so then he got his picture in the paper—a picture of him surrounded by animals, handing over his check to Venice Dudley, the manager of the shelter.

"I couldn't be more proud," Perry had said to Florence as he cut the photo out of the Wednesday edition of the *Little Spring Valley Weekly News and Ledger.*

"Della and Peony have never been in the paper," added his wife.

Since Egmont was in fact a very nice boy, he waited a full week after the night he asked his parents twenty-two times for a pet before he asked again. This time he thought he might ask fifty times. If his parents still said no, at least he would have the material he needed to write a story called "They Said No Fifty Times."

"Mom? Dad?" said Egmont as the Dolittles were finishing dinner. He swung his legs back and forth under his chair.

"Yes?" said Florence and Perry. They glanced at each other and smiled, since they knew what was coming.

"Can I get a pet?"

There was a pause. Then Florence replied, "What kind of pet do you have in mind?"

Egmont said "Can I get a pet?" again before he realized what his mother had asked him. Then he was so surprised that he dropped his fork to the floor and had to bend down to retrieve it before exclaiming, "What?!"

"What kind of pet do you have in mind?" Florence repeated.

Egmont's mouth dropped open. "Well . . . how about a horse?"

Mrs. Dolittle saw her husband's face go pale, but all he said was, "How about a fish?"

"Horse," said Egmont.

"Fish."

"Horse."

"Fish."

"Horse."

"Fish."

Egmont's parents sagged in their chairs. Mrs. Dolittle tried to recall Missy Piggle-Wiggle's phone number.

Across the table, Caramel cleared her throat. Her parents looked at her hopefully.

"Do you want any other kind of pet?" Caramel asked her brother. "Does it have to be a horse? I don't think we have room for a horse in our yard."

"Hmm." Egmont swirled his mashed potatoes around and arranged a grouping of peas in the middle of them.

"How about a cat?" suggested Caramel. The Free-foralls, who lived two doors away on the *other* side of the LaCartes, had a puffy-tailed cat named Muffet.

"Or, hey! How about a dog?" exclaimed Egmont, as if the idea had just occurred to him.

Caramel looked appealingly at her parents.

Her parents looked nervously at each other.

"A dog . . ." repeated Mr. Dolittle.

"A dog . . ." repeated Mrs. Dolittle.

"You do know that a dog is a lot of work," said Mr. Dolittle, at the very same time that Egmont said, "I know a dog is a lot of work."

"A dog needs to be fed and walked," added his mother.

"In all kinds of weather," agreed Egmont. "Yes, I know."

"And a dog needs to be bathed and groomed," said his father.

"Bathing a dog would be fun!" said Egmont. He was picturing something he had seen on television once— a large tin tub in someone's backyard, the tub overflowing with soapsuds, in the middle of which sat a happy, cooperative, sudsy dog.

"A dog needs to be trained," his mother went on.

"We could help with that," said Caramel.

"You do know," said Mr. Dolittle, "that when you walk a dog and it poops, you have to clean up the poop. You can't just leave it on the sidewalk."

Egmont frowned slightly, but then he put a smile on his face and said, "I promise that if we get a dog, I will do everything. I'll feed it and walk it and bathe it and clean up the poop. Everything," he said again.

"Maybe we could borrow a dog," spoke up Caramel.

"What?" said Mr. and Mrs. Dolittle and Egmont. They looked slightly alarmed.

"Maybe we could take care of Dottie sometime. You know, Beaufort Crumpet's dog? Just to see how it goes?"

"Oh! What a wonderful idea, Carrie. You're always thinking," said her mother.

～～～～

By now it should be apparent that Egmont had never wanted a horse in the first place. He'd wanted a dog all along. So he was overjoyed when his parents arranged for Dottie, a small, gray, floppy-eared dog who was just as polite as Lester the pig, to spend a weekend at their house. Beaufort walked her there, and when he arrived, he handed Egmont a roll of paper. He let it unfurl, and Egmont watched as it stopped just inches above the ground.

"What's that?" asked Egmont.

"Instructions for taking care of Dottie."

Egmont looked at the paper. It was a schedule, and it began:

7:00—walk Dottie outside until she pees

7:15—breakfast—½ can Petmore Chicken-In-Gravy with one scoop Petmore dry food

7:30—walk Dottie outside until she poops

The schedule went on and on and on. Then Beaufort handed Egmont a large shopping bag. Egmont peered inside. "And what's all *this*?"

"Pooper scoop, poop bags, food, leash, toys, blankie, towel for muddy paws, Daisy Fresh cleaner in case she has an accident . . ." Beaufort ticked the items off on his fingers.

"Wow," murmured Egmont.

"Yikes," said Caramel.

Beaufort knelt down and put his arms around Dottie. "You be a good girl this weekend, okay?" Dottie licked Beaufort's nose. Beaufort turned to Egmont. "Call me if you have any problems," he said.

Egmont did not have a single problem with Dottie. He followed the schedule to the minute.

"I'm impressed!" Florence Dolittle said to her son at the end of the weekend.

"That was a lot of work, and you were very responsible," added Perry.

"You walked Dottie in the rain," said Florence.

"You came home early from the Freeforalls' to give Dottie her dinner," said Perry.

"You scooped up poop and carried it home," said Caramel. "In front of all your friends!"

~~~~~

It was decided that Egmont was responsible enough to care for a dog of his own. The very next weekend, the Dolittles hopped in their car and drove to Friends Furrever. Venice Dudley recognized Egmont and gave the Dolittles a personal tour of the shelter. They walked up and down the corridors in the dog wing, looking at Chihuahuas and sheepdogs and mutts, spotted dogs and brown dogs and golden dogs, frightened dogs and yappy dogs and happy dogs.

"It's so hard to choose," said Egmont after half an hour. "Could we get two?"

"No."

"Okay."

An hour and a half after that, Egmont had made his decision. "That one," he said, pointing to a brown-and-white dog whose cage card read: *My name is Sunny. I'm two years old. I'm already trained, and I'm very sweet. I like children and other dogs, but I'm not fond of cats. Will you give me a home?*

The Dolittles drove Sunny to her new home. "Remember," Florence said to Egmont as they climbed out of the car, "Sunny is your dog, so she's your responsibility."

"I know!" he replied. "Come on, Sunny. I'll show you around."

The first weekend with Sunny went very well.

"I'm so proud of Egmont," said Mr. Dolittle on Sunday night. "We haven't had to lift a finger."

Egmont had fed Sunny, carefully following the directions from Friends Furrever. He had walked her on a schedule, as Beaufort had recommended. He had scooped her poop and deposited it in the trash can in the garage. He had played with Sunny and brushed her and hugged her, and Sunny had rewarded him by sleeping on his bed at night.

"Look at them," whispered his mother, peering into the darkened bedroom on Sunday evening. "Angels, both of them."

Six days went by. When Mr. Dolittle met Mr. Crumpet in the grocery store the next weekend, he said, "Thank you so much for letting us borrow Dottie. Egmont is doing splendidly with Sunny. He's a champion feeder, groomer, and walker. Why, I don't think the LaCarte girls could care for a dog any better."

Beaufort's father set a head of broccoli in his cart. "That's great news," he replied.

Mr. Dolittle knew it was probably bad luck to compare Egmont to Peony and Della, but he couldn't help himself. He was too proud of Egmont.

Not half an hour later, Mr. Dolittle drove into his garage, walked inside to the kitchen, slipped in a puddle on the floor, and dropped the three bags of groceries he'd been carrying.

Mrs. Dolittle came hurrying downstairs. "What on earth?" she cried. "What was that crash?" She found her husband sprawled on the floor, surrounded by broken eggs and rolling oranges.

Mr. Dolittle rubbed his elbow. "I slipped in . . ." He glanced around. "I slipped in . . . whatever that is." He leaned over to examine the puddle. "I think Sunny had an accident," he said.

"Well, that's odd," his wife replied. "Egmont has been sticking to the schedule."

"Really? Where is he?"

"Over at the Freeforalls'." She paused. "And he's been there for hours!" She stepped out into the backyard, cupped her hands around her mouth, and shouted, "Egmont!" She ignored the fact that in the yard between the Freeforalls' and hers, Della and Peony, wearing spotless yellow dresses, were sitting primly on lawn chairs, reading. "Egmont!" she yelled again.

From two yards away she heard an answering, "What?"

"Come home right now!"

Egmont returned home, full of apologies, and cleaned up Sunny's accident with Daisy Fresh. Then he cleaned up the broken eggs and put away whatever groceries could be saved. "I promise it will never happen again," he said to his parents.

"I hope not," said Florence. "Your poor father. And poor Sunny."

The next morning, which was Sunday, Egmont overslept. He lay in bed while Mr. and Mrs. Dolittle and Caramel sat in the kitchen eating breakfast, and Sunny stared first at them and then at her empty food bowl.

"I can't stand it anymore," Florence finally said, and she fed Sunny.

Later, Egmont neglected to brush Sunny when she came inside with burrs in her fur. Then he began to find excuses not to walk her. "The walks are boring!" he exclaimed on Monday. "All I do is stand around and wait for her to pee." On Tuesday, he claimed to be tired. On Wednesday, he said he wanted to play video games instead.

Mrs. Dolittle found herself saying "Poor Sunny" over and over again. "She misses her friend," she added, glancing at Egmont, who was lying on the couch in front of the television.

"What friend?" asked Egmont.

"*You!*" said his exasperated mother.

Egmont let out a sigh and continued watching TV.

"You do realize, don't you," said Mrs. Dolittle, "that Sunny is sitting by the door with her tennis ball in her mouth?"

Egmont grunted.

His mother went outside to play with Sunny.

That night, Mrs. Dolittle waited until Egmont and Caramel were asleep, and then she said solemnly to her husband, "Things have come to a head."

Mr. Dolittle nodded. He didn't have to ask what she meant. He had been the one to walk Sunny that evening, and his wife had been the one to feed her dinner.

"It is time," Florence Dolittle said slowly, "to call upon Missy Piggle-Wiggle."

Mr. Dolittle nodded again. "I'll take care of it." He dialed Missy's number.

Across town, Missy was enjoying a pleasant evening with Harold. They were seated at the dining room table in the upside-down house playing Scrabble with Lester. When the phone rang, Lester jumped up to grab it and Penelope screeched "Announce yourself!" into the receiver while Lester was passing the phone to Missy, so that Mr. Dolittle felt somewhat flustered when Missy finally said, "Hello?"

"Yes, well, hello," stammered Perry Dolittle. He introduced himself, then said, "Our son Egmont wanted a pet in the worst way, so finally we adopted a lovely dog named Sunny, but now—"

Missy interrupted him to say, "Ah. You must need the Won't-Walk-the-Dog Cure."

"Well, yes, I suppose we do. How did you know?"

"It's a common-enough problem. Nothing to worry about. Could you bring Sunny over tomorrow morning while Egmont is at school?"

"Sunny?"

"Yes, Sunny."

"All right."

Mr. Dolittle hung up the phone feeling perplexed. "I hope she knows what she's doing."

"Oh, I'm certain she does," said his wife. "She cured all of the Freeforall children."

~~~~~

The next morning, Mr. Dolittle walked Sunny to the upside-down house, since she needed the exercise. They hurried through town and then along the crooked little path to the front door with its two knobs. Above him, Serena Clutter was hammering away at a window frame. She waved to him while he gaped at the tarps covering the roof. He was about to ring the bell when the same raucous voice he'd heard the night before shrieked, "Missy, Mr. Dolittle and Sunny are here!"

Missy Piggle-Wiggle, wearing a strange flowing outfit that seemed to waft silver mist and sparkles into the air when she moved, greeted him, holding a biscuit in one hand.

"Let's see if Sunny will eat this," she said. Then she chuckled. "My friend Harold suggested that I give Egmont a dose of the Promise Potion, but I really don't see what that would accomplish. Here, Sunny. Have a treat."

Sunny stretched her neck toward Missy and took the biscuit delicately. She crunched it between her teeth and swallowed.

"That should do it," said Missy.

Perry Dolittle frowned, feeling more perplexed than ever.

"Starting right now," Missy went on, "put Sunny in charge of Egmont, rather than the other way around."

"Put *Sunny* in charge? Well . . . all right."

Mr. Dolittle began the walk home. He had almost reached Juniper Street when he noticed that Sunny's front paws were rising above the sidewalk and she was trundling along on her back legs. She looked over her shoulder at Mr. Dolittle and waved at him with her right front paw. By the time they were approaching the other end of Juniper Street, Sunny was walking fully upright on her hind legs. Mr. Dolittle was surprised at how tall she was. The leash seemed sort of unnecessary. He felt as though he were walking a friend on a leash, so he unclipped it.

"Thank you," said Sunny.

They passed A to Z Books, and Sunny waved through the window to Harold. She waited for Mr. Dolittle to catch up to her, and as they walked along side by side, she said, "Maybe I'll take Egmont to the bookstore one day." Then she added, "In case Missy didn't make it clear, when she said that I'll be responsible for Egmont, she meant that I'll be giving him his meals, doing his laundry—everything."

"My" was all Mr. Dolittle managed to reply.

~~~~~

It shouldn't come as a surprise to learn that Egmont was delighted to return from school that afternoon

and find that he had a talking dog. "I'm going to show you off to everyone!" he announced to Sunny.

"Let me fix you a snack first," Sunny replied. "I don't want you going out to play on an empty stomach."

Mrs. Dolittle and Caramel watched in fascination as Sunny expertly made an open-faced peanut-butter-and-banana-sandwich and placed it in front of Egmont.

"Could I have one, too, please?" asked Caramel.

"Certainly."

After snack time, Sunny, Egmont, and Caramel went to the Freeforalls'. (They took a shortcut through the LaCartes' yard. Della shrieked when she saw Sunny walking tall between Egmont and Caramel, holding each one by the hand, and she fled into her house.)

"Look what I have," said Egmont when Frankfort answered the Freeforalls' door. "A talking dog-person."

"Cool," replied Frankfort.

That night, just as Missy had promised, Sunny took complete charge of Egmont. She made him his dinner, which was a lucky thing, since Mr. Dolittle was preparing artichokes and when Egmont saw them he cried, "I will not eat food with thorns on it!" Sunny fixed him chicken nuggets instead. Later she sat patiently by his side while he did his homework and checked the spelling in his composition titled "Sunny, the Talking Dog." She reminded him to brush his teeth, and she read a chapter from *Danny, the Champion of the World* to him before he fell asleep.

The next morning, Sunny fixed Egmont's breakfast and walked him and Caramel to school.

"Will you come inside with me?" asked Egmont at the door.

"If you'd like me to." Sunny walked Egmont to his class and stayed by his side all day, making Egmont the most popular kid at Little Spring Valley Elementary, since no one else had ever brought a talking dog to school.

That afternoon, when Sunny asked Egmont what he'd like to do, he said, "Can we go to the upside-down house?"

"Certainly," replied Sunny, which was another lucky thing, because Egmont and Caramel weren't allowed to cross streets by themselves. Sunny called to Mr. Dolittle, who was working in his home office, "I'm taking the children to Missy Piggle-Wiggle's!" and off they went.

It was a dreary, rainy, end-of-spring day, the kind of

day most grown-ups dread. The Dolittles dreaded those days because Egmont and Caramel would whine, "What are we supposed to *do* with ourselves? There's nothing to *do* indoors. We want to go out*side*."

Missy Piggle-Wiggle, the only grown-up at the upside-down house, never minded rainy days. When bored, whiny children showed up, she would suggest that they find new ways of jumping on the couch, or she would show them how to make invisible ink. On this rainy day, Egmont found eight children at Missy's having indoor relay races. He and Caramel joined in, and Sunny cheered them on. "Way to go, Egmont!" she called from the sidelines. "Good try, Carrie!"

They walked home at the end of the afternoon, Sunny holding a large umbrella over the Dolittle children. Egmont looked forward to the dinner Sunny had promised to fix for him: eggs and pancakes. "BFD," Sunny informed him. "Breakfast for Dinner. The best kind of meal."

Egmont went to sleep that night with a smile on his face. Sunny slept soundly beside him.

The next morning, the rain had ended. Egmont bounded out of bed. "Sun's out!" he announced. He opened his bureau drawer. "Hey, I don't have any underwear."

Sunny rolled onto her side and pulled a pillow over her head. "I guess I forgot to do your laundry," she murmured.

Egmont said, "Oh." He looked around his room. "What should I wear instead?"

"How about your bathing suit?"

"Okay, I guess. Will you do my laundry today?"

"Sure."

Egmont dressed himself in a shirt and a pair of shorts over his SpongeBob bathing trunks. He could hear Sunny snoring underneath the covers. He checked the time. "Um, Sunny?" he said. "It's a school day. I need to eat breakfast now."

"Okay, go ahead."

"But aren't you supposed to make it for me?"

"I'm a little tired."

Egmont walked slowly down the stairs and fixed himself a bowl of cereal. He missed having Sunny seated next to him at the table.

Sunny did get up in time to walk Egmont and Caramel to school, but she left them at the door.

"I guess you have a lot to do today," Egmont said to her.

"What? Oh, right. Your laundry and so forth."

Egmont felt funny all morning. He tried to identify the feeling. He didn't feel sick exactly, although his stomach didn't feel quite right. His thoughts kept drifting to Sunny, the Sunny who would play with him and read to him and fix him BFD. He was actually glad when his teacher announced at the end of the day that they were going to have a spelling test the next morning.

"Sunny!" Egmont said breathlessly. He was relieved to find her waiting in front of Little Spring Valley Elementary. "We have a big test tomorrow. Our teacher just announced it. Will you help me study for it tonight? I need someone to quiz me."

"Hmm," said Sunny. "I don't know. There's a *Dog Whisperer* marathon on TV."

Egmont walked along in silence between Sunny and his sister. Finally he said, "Um, Sunny, did you do the laundry today?"

"No. Why?"

"Well, my bathing suit isn't very comfortable."

Sunny clapped her front paw to her forehead. "Laundry is so boring! Maybe you can do the laundry."

"But I have to study for the test."

"All right, I'll try to get around to it."

At home that afternoon, Sunny handed Egmont a peach for a snack and settled in front of the TV.

"Want to play catch before I start studying?" Egmont asked her.

Sunny wrinkled her snout and shook her head.

Egmont went to his room and sat at his desk. He opened his book and tried to concentrate on spelling *discipline* and *responsibility*, but his mind kept wandering. Egmont might have been bright, but he hadn't wondered until right that very minute how Sunny had turned from an ordinary dog into a walking, talking dog. The more he thought about it, the more he felt that Missy Piggle-Wiggle might have had something to do with the transformation. After all, she was the one who had put Frankfort Freeforall into the giant Bubble of Apology to help him learn to think about others. And she was the one who had given Linden Pettigrew that disgusting magic gum ball to help with his gum smacking.

Egmont crept downstairs. Sunny was stretched out on the couch with a bowl of popcorn. The TV was blaring. "I'm going out," he called to her.

"Bye!" Sunny replied.

Egmont wasn't allowed to walk to Missy's by himself, so he went to the Freeforalls' and asked Honoriah if she would walk with him to the upside-down house. "I have to cross streets with an adult," he told her.

Honoriah, who was nine, was thrilled to be considered an adult. "Let's go," she said.

Egmont was dismayed to find a whole yardful of children at Missy's house. He needed a private moment with her. "Missy?" he said.

Missy looked up from the geraniums she and Melody were planting in one of the many holes in the lawn. (She was transplanting the flowers from the backyard to the front yard since she couldn't afford to buy new ones.) "Oh, Egmont. I expect you need to talk to me," she said.

"Yes," Egmont replied, not feeling even a little surprised.

"Let's go into the kitchen."

Egmont and Missy sat at the table with cups of ice water. Egmont stared at his cup and swung his feet until Missy said, "Egmont?"

"I think I broke Sunny!" he suddenly exclaimed. His chin quivered. "You gave me a talking dog, and everything was great at first, but then Sunny just . . . She just . . ."

"Forgot about you?" suggested Missy.

"Sort of," said Egmont miserably. "She won't play with me or take care of me or anything."

"I suppose you feel as though you've lost a friend."

Egmont nodded again. He remembered his mother saying to him that Sunny missed her friend. And Egmont, lost in a TV show, had actually replied, "What friend?"

Egmont dropped his head onto his arms and bawled. "Sunny sat at the door with her tennis ball in her mouth, and I ignored her because something was on"—he let out a loud sob—"because something was on"—sob, sob—"something was ON TV!" Sob, sob, sob, sob.

"Goodness me," said Missy. "What do you think we should do?"

"All I want is Sunny back. The old Sunny, my friend. The talking Sunny is fun, but I want the Sunny who would chase me around the yard—on four legs—and who licked my face when I fed her and then breathed dog-food breath on me."

"You do know that's the same Sunny you have to walk several times a day—"

"And clean up after. I know." Egmont's sobs had subsided, and he began to sniffle. Missy handed him a tissue. "Can you help me?" he asked.

"Of course." Missy reached into a jar that Egmont could have sworn wasn't there a moment earlier. She pulled out an ordinary-looking dog biscuit. "Give this to Sunny when you get home."

"Thank you, Missy," said Egmont. Then he leaped out of his chair and yelled, "Honoriah, we have to go home RIGHT NOW!"

~~~~~

That night, Harold Spectacle and Missy sat on the front porch of the upside-down house and looked at the stars in the sky. He could hear the tarp flapping softly in the breeze.

"What did you do today?" asked Harold. Missy always had the most interesting answers to this question.

"I returned Sunny to her dog self."

"So Egmont is cured?"

"I believe so."

"How long did the cure take?"

"Just a few days."

"Your cures are so . . . meaningful," said Harold. "Once my teacher made me write 'I will not talk in class' one hundred times on the blackboard."

"Did that teach you not to talk in class?"

"Nope. It just made me hate chalk."

"Naturally."

Missy was very, very wise, Harold thought. He reached for her hand, and they sat for a long time under the stars.

Across town, Egmont took Sunny into the yard for her last walk before bedtime. Sunny leaped up and down beside him as they returned to the house. Then she rushed upstairs and curled herself into a ball on Egmont's bed.

Egmont slept soundly next to his best friend all night.

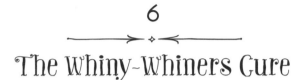

6

The Whiny-Whiners Cure

ON A BRIGHT morning in late June, Mr. and Mrs. Ferdinand Forthright looked at each other across the breakfast table and clasped hands.

"It's here," whispered Alexa, Ferdinand's wife.

"What we've been dreading," replied her husband.

"Ten weeks. Ten. *Weeks.*"

"Day after day after day. Why does summer vacation have to be so long?"

"I'm going to put in a call to Valerian Hoonley this morning," announced Alexa. She let go of her husband's hands and straightened up, trying to will herself to feel brave.

"Who's Valerian Hoonley?"

"You know Mrs. Hoonley," Alexa replied, which was ridiculous, because if her husband knew who Valerian Hoonley was, he wouldn't have said, "Who's Valerian Hoonley?"

"I really don't."

"She lives across the street and two houses down."

"Oh. Why are you going to call her?"

"Because she's the only neighbor I've met since we moved to Little Spring Valley. And because her children never whine. Maybe she'll have some advice for us about Austin and Houston."

Mr. Forthright put his hands to his temples and closed his eyes. The very mention of his children gave him a small headache. Suddenly he opened his eyes. He had heard a noise from upstairs. He pushed his chair away from the table and grabbed his briefcase. "I'd better get to the office." He rushed out the door just as his children came thundering down the stairs.

"MO-OOOOOOM! WHERE ARE MY SNEAKERS? I CAAAAAN'T FIIIIIND MY SNEAKERS!" whined Austin. She thrust herself into her chair. "THIS IS THE

WROOOOOOONG KIIIIIND OF JAAAAAM!" she added. "WHERE'S THE RAAAAAASPBERRY?"

Houston flung himself down next to his sister. "WHAT ARE WE GOING TO DOOOOOO TODAA-AAAAY? WE HAVE A WHOLE DAAAAY WITH NOTHING TO DOOOOOOOOOOOOOOO." He poked out his lower lip.

Mrs. Forthright looked longingly out the window, where she could see her husband backing his car down the driveway. He was so lucky that he got to spend the entire day in an office. She sighed and found Austin's sneakers and the raspberry jam.

"YOU DIDN'T ANSWER MEEEEEE," whined Houston. "I SAAAAID, WHAT ARE WE GOING TO DOOOOO TODAY?"

His mother lowered her voice, which she hoped would encourage her son to do the same, but this had never, ever worked. "You could walk to school and play on the playground," she whispered. The school was half a mile from their house. Surely her children's whiny voices couldn't carry that far.

Austin moaned, "BUT WHAT IF IT RAAAAA-AAAINS?" She said this without bothering to turn around and look out the window. If she had, she would have seen the lovely sunshiny day and the clear blue sky.

"I don't think it's supposed to rain today," murmured her mother.

Houston sat on his chair and stared at the jar of raspberry jam. Then he stuck his finger in it. "THERE ARE BROOOOOOWN THINGS IN HEEE-EEEERE."

"MOM, HE PUT HIS FIIIIIINGER IN THE JAAAAAAAM!" cried Austin. "THAT IS DIS. GUS. TIIIIIIIIING."

Mrs. Forthright scooped out a spoonful of the offending jam. She turned to Houston. "The brown things are raspberry seeds."

"BUT I DON'T LIIIIIIKE SEEDS IN MY JAAAAAAM. THEY GET CAUGHT IN MY TEEEEE-EEEEEEEEEEEEEEETH. I CAN'T EEEEEAT THIS."

Mrs. Forthright stepped out of the kitchen. She stepped all the way on to the front porch, where she stood for a moment, breathing deeply. Across the street, that nice neighbor whose name was either Mr. Bickle or Mr. Buckle was watering the flower garden with his two small sons. Alexa breathed in, out, in, out, relishing the peace. At last, with great reluctance, she turned around and listened at her front door. All was quiet, so she went back inside. The moment she appeared in the kitchen doorway, Austin said, "MO-OOOOOOM, IT IS SOOOOOOOOO HAAAAAAAARD BEING THE NEW KID!"

"WHY DID WE HAVE TO MOOOOOOOVE HEEEEEERE?" added Houston. "WE DON'T KNOW ANYBODYYYYYYYYYYYYYY."

"You've been going to school in Little Spring Valley for two months," their mother replied. "And, Austin, you've been going to dance class for almost as long. You must have met plenty of kids, both of you."

"NOBODY LIIIIIIIIKES US," whined Houston.

"THEY'RE ALL STUCK UUUUUUUUUP," added Austin.

"They can't possibly *all* be stuck up. Why don't you each invite a friend over today?"

"WE ALREADY TOOOOOOOLD YOU," said Houston. "WE DON'T KNOOOOOOOW ANYBODY."

"WE HAAAAAAVE NO FRIEEEEEEENDS," added Austin.

"Just one person each. A classmate. Surely you know some of your classmates." Alexa Forthright paused to sigh. "And could you please lower your voices a bit? I'm four feet away. I can hear you just fine."

Austin set down her glass of orange juice. She was a thin, pale girl who found so many faults with the food her parents served her that she rarely finished a meal. Now she leaned over to get a better look at her juice. "THERE'S PULP IN HEEEEEEERE! I CAN'T STAAAAAAND PULP!" She pushed the glass away.

"I HATE SEEDS," Houston said again.

"Friends," their mother reminded them. "What about inviting some kids over today? I'll make the phone calls for you. Austin, who should I call for you?"

Austin let out a sigh big enough to have come from a whale. At last, she said in a wispy little voice, "Petulance Freeforall."

"Great. And Houston, who should I call for you?"

Houston buried his head in his hands and muttered, "Egmont Dolittle. But he won't come."

This is how Mrs. Forthright's phone calls went:

MRS. FORTHRIGHT: Hello, I'm looking for Petulance Freeforall.

PETULANCE: That's me.

MRS. FORTHRIGHT: I'm Austin Forthright's mother, and I was wondering if you'd like to—

PETULANCE: I can't. I'm busy today. I'm busy all the days. Bye!

MRS. FORTHRIGHT: But I didn't even tell you . . . Hello? Hello? . . . *Hello?*

"She hung up, didn't she?" said Austin. "I knew it." She tipped her head to the ceiling and closed her eyes. "STUUUUUUUCK UUUUUUP. Just like I said."

Her mother was undeterred. "Let me try Egmont." She punched in the number on her phone.

EGMONT: Hello, Dolittle residence.

MRS. FORTHRIGHT: Egmont? What lovely manners you have. This is Mrs. Forthright, Houston's mother.

EGMONT: Ummmmmmm . . .

MRS. FORTHRIGHT: Egmont? Are you still there?

EGMONT: I have to go walk my dog. . . . Take care!

Mrs. Forthright ended the call. She really couldn't blame Petulance and Egmont. If she were a kid, *she* wouldn't want to play with Austin or Houston.

She looked at her children. Austin had taken four sips from her pulpy orange juice and several miniscule bites from the middle of her toast, leaving a large pile of remains on her plate. Houston had eaten around every single raspberry seed on his toast, leaving behind a billion teensy pieces of toast, each with one seed in the middle. "Can't you think of a single thing to do today?" asked Mrs. Forthright.

Austin let out another one of her whale sighs. "Lots of kids around here go to Missy Piggle-Wiggle's house."

"Who's Missy Piggle-Wiggle?"

"That funny lady who lives in the upside-down house with the barn in back."

"Oh. I was wondering who that house belongs to. Why do the kids like to visit her?"

"She has lots of pets. A cat and a dog and a talking parrot."

"She's supposed to be magic."

Mrs. Forthright frowned. "Are you certain about that?"

"YEEEEEEEES!" cried Austin, who wasn't certain at all, since she had never met Missy, let alone visited the upside-down house.

"This person is a magician?" asked her mother.

"NO!" Houston kicked his shoes furiously against the legs of his chair. "She's MAAAAAAGIC, not a magician."

"What exactly makes her magic?"

"Um, her clothes, I think," Austin replied weakly.

"She has a pet pig," added Houston, who would have sounded more impressed if he had actually met Lester and watched him prepare a meal.

"And the kids here like to visit her?"

"YEEEEEES! WE ALREADY TOOOOOOLD YOU!" wailed Austin.

Houston kicked at his chair again.

"Can you please stop that, dear?" said his mother.

"I WASN'T DOING ANYTHIIIIIIING! WHY ARE YOU ALWAYS CRITICIZING ME?"

Alexa Forthright did a quick calculation and figured that the upside-down house was at least a mile away. "Why don't you two visit Mrs. Piggly-Wiggly today?"

"THAT'S NOT EVEN HER NAAAAAAAAME!" cried Austin. "It's *Missy Piggle-Wiggle*."

"Apologies. Missy Piggle-Wiggle. Why don't you walk over there? It's a beautiful day—"

"CAN'T YOU DRIIIIIIIIVE US?" whined Austin.

"I could, but you need some exercise. Go on. It's the first day of summer vacation. Enjoy yourselves."

~~~~~

Across town at the upside-down house, breakfast was over. Missy had risen early and done the morning farm chores. She had fed Wag and Lightfoot and Penelope, and she had made a pot of coffee for Serena and her crew. The day was already warm, and Missy had opened the back door to let in the summer air and the scent of roses.

The moment should have been peaceful, but Missy was pacing the kitchen, staring at a piece of paper Serena had handed her earlier.

"What's this?" Missy had asked.

Serena had stared at the floor and shuffled her feet around. "A revised estimate for the repair job."

"Oh," said Missy. And then, when she'd looked at the figure at the bottom of the page, she'd added, "Oh, dear."

"I'm sorry," said Serena. "It's just that the work is taking longer than I thought it would."

Missy knew Serena was too polite to add that even

when the house was behaving, the job wasn't easy. The day before, for instance, Serena had had to pull out all the cabley things she had just installed because they were backward.

"They would be perfectly perfect in other buildings," Serena had said as she tugged and pulled at the wires. "But here, they're—"

"Wonky?" suggested Penelope in a loud voice, and the house had let out an alarming grumble.

Now, to add to Missy's worries, Penelope was swooping back and forth through the kitchen, emitting squawks and screeches.

"What on earth is the matter?" Missy asked her.

"Trouble! Trouble on the way!"

More trouble? wondered Missy.

The doorbell rang. Penelope flapped to the front door and announced, "Never mind. It's only Georgie Pepperpot and Veronica Cupcake!"

~~~~~

Alexa Forthright shut the door behind Houston and Austin and leaned against it briefly. Just as soon as she recovered from breakfast, she would put in a call to

Valerian Hoonley. She watched her children straggle down the sidewalk. Even with the front door closed tightly, she could hear Houston say, "I DON'T KNOW WHY MOM IS MAKING US GO OOOOOOVER THEEEEEERE."

"WE DON'T EVEN KNOOOOOOOW MISSY PIGGLE-WIGGLE."

"MOM IS SOOOOOO MEEEEEEEEAN."

"AND UNFAAAAAAAAIR." Austin slumped along, scuffing her sneakers down the sidewalk, leaving tiny bits of rubber in her wake.

Houston followed three paces behind. "STOP WALKING SO FAAAAAST. I CAN'T KEEP UP WITH YOOOOOOOU!"

"I'M NOT WALKING FAST; YOU'RE WALKING SLOOOOOW. YOU'RE A COMPLETE SLOOOOOOO-OOWPOKE."

By the time the Forthright children had whinily reached the upside-down house, they were sweaty and tragic-looking. They stood together at the end of the crooked path leading to the porch and glanced at each other.

"Should we really go in?" Austin asked her brother.
"All the other kids do."

"The house looks creepy. And there's a hole in the roof!"

"This place is weird." Austin cocked his head. "Did you hear that? Someone inside the house just said, 'Trouble! Trouble at our door!'"

"You're making things up."

The Forthrights stumbled along the path, which seemed to shift beneath their feet. They struggled to keep their balance. They had just reached the steps to the porch when suddenly every single window shade in the house flapped down. At the same time, the steps were slurped inside the house like a turtle drawing its head into its shell.

"Hey!" exclaimed Houston. "The steps disappeared! How are we supposed to get INSIIIIIIDE?"

"WE WALKED AAAAAAALL THE WAY OVER HERE FOR NOTHIIIIIIIING!"

The door was opened then by a young woman with the reddest hair Austin had ever seen. She was wearing a straw hat with a ribbon tied around the brim and a flowy, sparkly lavender dress that reached all the way down to her ankles. A parrot was perched on her shoulder, and a large pig stood at her side.

"You must be the Forthrights," said the woman. Then she called over her shoulder, "House, put yourself back to rights, please."

The house grumbled and moaned.

"No dawdling!" ordered Missy.

Austin looked at Houston in dismay and said in her quietest voice (which Missy could hear perfectly well), "She seems kind of mean." But then the porch steps unfurled and the window shades snapped up, and Missy smiled at her guests.

"Welcome," said Missy. "Let me see. You must be Austin." She pointed to Austin. "And you must be Houston." The Forthrights nodded. "Come on inside. Georgie and Veronica are here, and we're making blueberry muffins."

Houston rushed up the stairs, certain that they would disappear beneath his feet. Austin ran even faster, passed her brother on the porch, and stopped breathlessly in the hallway of the upside-down house.

"Whoa," she said.

Houston ran into her from behind. "Whoa," he said.

There was silence as they turned around and around, looking at the furniture that had floated to the ceiling and the chandeliers sprouting from the floor.

"How do you read?" Austin finally asked.

Missy waved her hand. "I just curl up on the floor by one of the lights."

Lester tugged at Missy, and she sniffed the air. "I think the muffins are done. Come join us in the kitchen."

Houston and Austin followed Missy Piggle-Wiggle and the pig to the kitchen, where two children they didn't know had strapped scrub brushes to their feet and were skating across the floor.

"Thank you for cleaning up," Missy said to them.

She was about to serve the muffins when the parrot squawked, "Melody Flowers is here!" Two minutes later she squawked, "Rusty and Tulip are here!" Two minutes after that, she squawked, "Harold Spectacle is here—even though it's a workday and he should be at the store!"

Soon the little kitchen was bursting with people and animals. Lester passed around a plate of muffins.

"Thank you, Lester," said Melody.

"Yes, thank you," said Rusty.

"Mmmm. These are scrumptious," said Veronica, who had just that morning learned what *scrumptious* meant.

Houston took a muffin and bit into it. He chewed. And then he spat the mouthful into his hand. "THEEEEEEESE HAVE SEEEEEEDS! I HAAAAA-AATE SEEDS."

"Blueberries don't have seeds," said Tulip. "They're too little."

"Of course they do. All fruits have seeds!" wailed Houston.

"Okay, but blueberry seeds are the size of, like, molecules," replied Tulip.

"I DON'T CAAAAAARE! I CRUNCHED ON ONE. I KNOW THEY'RE IN THE MUFFIIIIIINS!"

"Gracious," said Harold. "I think we should institute a no-whining rule."

Veronica was staring wide-eyed at Houston. "And a no-spitting rule," she said. "If you do that again, I'll barf."

"Rules like that aren't generally effective," murmured

Missy. Then she turned to Austin. "Would you like a muffin?"

Austin squinched up her eyes and whined, "BLUEBERRIES TURN MY TOOOOOOOOONGUE BLUUUUUUUUUE."

"Goodness," said Harold, who had sat down at the table next to Lester.

"Of course they turn your tongue blue," said Rusty, frowning. "They're *blue*berries."

"BUT I DON'T WAAAAAAANT A BLUE TOOOOOOOONGUE."

Melody took Austin by the hand. "You're new here, aren't you?" she said with great sympathy. "I was new here last year, and in my old town, Utopia—"

Tulip rolled her eyes. "We know, we know. Utopia was perfect."

"But in Utopia," Melody went on desperately, "there was an after-school club for . . ."

Harold stood up then and beckoned Missy into the living room. "I'd better get back to the store," he said. "I just wanted to stop by and say hello." He grabbed his top hat and ran for the door. "Do you by any chance have a cure for whining?" he asked.

"Absolutely. But I need to wait until one of the Forthright parents calls and asks me for help. A good cure must be timed just right."

Harold nodded and stroked his chin. Then he gave Missy a quick hug and left for the bookstore.

Missy returned to the kitchen just as Georgie said, "Let's go digging for pirate treasure," and Houston replied, "Digging for treasure? BUT IT'S HOOOOOOOT OUTSIDE!"

Missy noticed that her fingertips were beginning to tingle. She felt that one or the other of the Forthright parents would call her within three days. She wiggled her fingers. No, she thought. The call would come within three hours.

~~~~~~

Alexa Forthright drove to the grocery store and began the tedious process of choosing foods her children wouldn't object to. She was in the cereal aisle searching for something that didn't crunch too much but that also wouldn't get too soggy in milk, that was neither too sweet nor not sweet enough, that didn't smell like fruit or vanilla or cinnamon or chocolate, and that had almonds in it but no other kind of nut, because these were Austin's cereal requirements.

"Mrs. Forthright?" said a voice from behind her.

Alexa jumped. "Oh! It's . . . Mrs. Freeforall, isn't it?" Alexa had a dim memory of meeting Mrs. Freeforall one afternoon in the parking lot of Little Spring Valley Elementary School.

Mrs. Freeforall smiled. "Yes. How are things going? I know you're new here and that moving can be very stressful." Before Alexa could reply, Mrs. Freeforall barreled on, "I was wondering if you'd made the acquaintance of Missy Piggle-Wiggle."

"How odd that you should mention—"

"If you don't mind my saying so, I couldn't help but notice that your children have a bit of a problem with, well, whining. Now, Missy has cured all my children of . . . I'm not certain how else to say this . . . of *unwanted habits.*"

"She's a wonder!" said a man's voice from the canned-goods aisle. A head peeped around a display of tomato soup. "Missy cured my daughter Heavenly of her habit of being late for everything. Every. Single. Thing," he added. "I'm sure she could do something for your children."

"Really?" Alexa felt she should be offended that every parent she met seemed to know about Houston and Austin and their whining, but she was too relieved by the prospect of a cure for them—an actual *cure*—to be truly offended. Side by side, she and Mrs. Freeforall pushed their carts toward the checkout counter, where they bumped into nice Mr. Bickle or Buckle from across the way.

"I've been meaning to tell you," Mr. Bickle-Buckle began, "about a wonderful woman in town who might be able to do something about the whining I hear coming from your—"

Alexa Forthright held up her hand. "Does anybody have Missy Piggle-Wiggle's phone num—?"

"Yes!" cried Mrs. Freeforall, Mr. Bickle-Buckle, and Heavenly's father.

Alexa pulled out her cell phone.

At the upside-down house, the ringing phone was picked up by Lester, who handed it politely to Penelope, who squawked, "Hello? Hello? Hello?"

Alexa thought the voice sounded parrot-like, but she bravely asked for Missy Piggle-Wiggle. And when Missy found out who was calling, she said, "Ah. I've been expecting you. I'll send Austin and Houston home with"—she caught herself before she said "the Whiny-Whiners Cure"—"the perfect cure."

"Oh, couldn't you please give it to them now? *Right* now? I don't think my husband and I can wait one second longer. I hope it's fast acting."

"Very fast acting," Missy assured her.

Missy ended the call and hurried upstairs to her room. She opened the cure cabinet and surveyed the contents. The Whiny-Whiners Cure had edged itself to the front of the shelf so it would be easy to find. Missy carried the small box out to the front porch, where Austin and Houston were sitting like lumps. "I have a treat for you," she said. She shook two ruby-colored drops into her hand.

"What are they? Candy?" asked Austin. "I don't like anything blue or salty or slimy or too sweet or too sour."

"They don't have seeds, do they?" asked Houston.

"They're seedless, red, and delicious," said Missy.

Austin pinched one between her fingers and examined it suspiciously. Then she touched it to her tongue. "Hey, it's good!" she said. "Try yours, Houston."

Houston rolled his around in his mouth, frowning furiously. At last he said, "It *is* good."

"Wonderful," said Missy, and she sat back and waited.

Ten minutes later, Lester appeared at the front door. He pushed it open with a hind hoof and set down a tray with a stack of cups and a heavy pitcher.

"Lemonade!" shrieked Veronica, and she and the others ran for the porch, Wag at their heels.

Lester poured the lemonade into cups, and Georgie passed the cups around. He handed one to Austin, and she peered into it, then said, "I SEE PUUUUUUUULP!"

No one looked at her. No one paid even the slightest bit of attention. Lester kept pouring, and Georgie kept passing.

Austin set down her cup. "I SAAAAAAAID, I SEE PUUUUULP!"

Houston stared at his sister. "Are you saying something?" he asked.

Austin's face was turning red. She clenched her fists and tried again. "THERE'S PULP IN MY LE-MONADE!"

"Whoa," said Houston. "Your lips are moving, but no sound is coming out. It's like you're on mute."

"Really? That's so weird," said his sister.

"I heard you that time."

"Maybe I'm getting a cold and losing my voice. Or else it's probably the *pulp* in the lemonade. I HAAAATE—"

"Are you still talking?" asked her brother. "Because you're on mute again."

"Hey, Houston," said Rusty a few minutes later. "Are you sure you don't want to dig for treasure with us? One day we're going to find it, you know. The very next hole could be the one with the treasure chest at the bottom."

Houston rolled his eyes. "There's no treasure. And besides, IT'S SOOOOOO—"

Rusty looked at Houston, whose mouth was working furiously but who suddenly wasn't making a sound. He knocked on Houston's head. "Hello? Anybody home?"

What Houston was trying to say was, "IT'S SOOOOOOOO HOT OUT HERE! I'LL FAAAAAA-AINT. AND BESIDES, DIGGING FOR TREASURE IS FOR BAAAAAAABIES." He could hear himself inside his head.

But Rusty heard absolutely nothing.

Houston grabbed for his sister's hand and whispered to her, "We have to get out of here. Something weird is going on."

"It must be this house," Austin replied. She glanced behind her at the window, and the shade snapped down, then up. Lester smiled at her.

The Forthrights, still hand in hand, jumped down the steps and ran for the street.

"Hey, don't you want to finish your scrumptious lemonade?" Veronica called after them.

Houston and Austin didn't stop running until they had turned a corner and could no longer see the upside-down house. They slowed to a walk and caught their breath.

"Do I have a fever?" Austin asked her brother.

He put a hand to her forehead. "I don't think so.

Let's just get home." They walked silently until they reached their front door. Then they barged inside, where they found their mother unpacking groceries.

Alexa Forthright sighed. "Back so soon?"

"Mom, it was *horrible* there!" Houston cried. "Everyone was MEAN, AND THIS PIIIIIIIG—"

Mrs. Forthright stared at her son. She could see that he was speaking—that, in fact, he was quite worked up about something—but no sound was coming out of his mouth.

The relief that washed over her caused her to sink into a chair.

"Do you hear him, Mom?" asked Austin. "Maybe we're going deaf."

"I don't think we're going deaf, dear."

"But something is WROOOOOONG!" wailed Austin. "SOMETHING HAPPENED AT THAT HOUUUUUUUUSE—"

Mrs. Forthright smiled. Now she could hear neither of her children. "How about some lunch?" she asked brightly.

Austin rolled her tongue around in her mouth. She

swallowed several times. Experimentally, she said, "Ah-ah-ah-ah-*ah*-ah-ah-ah-ah," like a singer warming up. Then she asked, "Can you hear me now?"

"Perfectly," said her mother.

"Can you hear *me*?" asked Houston.

Their mother nodded. "I'll make grilled cheese sandwiches."

"GRILLED CHEEEEEEEESE? I DON'T WANT—" Austin's voice was cut off as if someone had snipped a wire.

Inside her head, Alexa Forthright was saying, *Thank you, Missy. Thank you, Missy. Thank you, wonderful, magical Missy Piggle-Wiggle, whoever you are.*

~~~~~

That afternoon, Mrs. Forthright attempted something she usually never, ever did unless her husband could come along. She took Houston and Austin shoe shopping. Shoe shopping caused whining of unimaginable proportions. Whining about pinched toes and ugly colors and the fact that everyone else's parents let them wear sparkles.

But Alexa was feeling brave. She marched her

children into Heel to Toe and said to the salesman, "We need sneakers, please. Sensible sneakers that will last into the fall at least."

"SENSI—" Austin started to whine. In her head she was saying, "SENSIBLE? I DON'T WANT SENSIBLE SHOES! I WANT SPAAAAARKLES!" but she had a feeling no sound was issuing from her mouth.

Sure enough, the salesman, whose nametag read MR. CARBUNKLE, was staring at her as if, Austin thought, she had something green on one of her teeth and he couldn't decide whether to mention it.

Now, sometimes parents make very bad mistakes in the rearing of their children. For instance, sometimes they rear children who are whiners, or children who would be allowed to mock them simply for saying the word *rear*. But other times they have epiphanies, which is a scholarly way of saying that suddenly they have helpful insights regarding thorny problems. That's exactly what happened to Alexa Forthright on that warm June afternoon in Heel to Toe on Juniper Street.

It suddenly occurred to her to take advantage of the fact that her children were magically incapable of whining. "Austin," she said, "do you have a different idea about your sneakers? Maybe you can you tell Mr. Carbunkle what you'd like—in a clear, calm manner."

Austin swallowed. She took a deep breath. And then she found herself saying, "I was hoping for sparkles on my shoes. Do you have any sneakers that are practical *and* sparkly?"

"Absolutely," replied Mr. Carbunkle. He turned to Houston. "And for you, sir?"

Houston had been staring openmouthed at his sister. It was on the tip of his tongue to say, "THIS IS GOING TO TAKE FOREEEEEEVER, AND I WANT TO GO HOOOOOOOME." Instead he said, "Mom, can't we go home now? Please?"

Alexa shook her head. "No. You need sneakers. But the more you cooperate, the sooner we'll get home."

The Forthrights set a record that afternoon. They were in and out of the shoe store in less than half an hour. As they walked to their car, Austin said in awe, "Mr. Carbunkle was right. He found sparkly, practical sneakers. And they fit just fine."

"Well, you were very cooperative," replied her mother. "You answered his questions—"

"I know," interrupted Austin. "In a clear, calm manner."

"And it paid off. Houston, I know you wanted to go straight home, but how about if we stop for ice cream first?"

"Ice cream? In the middle of the day?"

"As a reward for the lovely way you both interacted with Mr. Carbunkle."

The trip to Fester's for ice cream was as successful as the trip to Heel to Toe. When Mr. Fester accidentally handed Houston's cone to Austin, and Austin began to shriek, "THAT ONE HAS CHOCO—" Houston simply reached for it and said, "Thank you. The other cone is my sister's." Then he whispered to Austin, "The adults respond better if you don't panic. Just go with it."

The only glitch in the Forthrights' Whiny-Whiners Cure came when Mr. Forthright, unaware of the events of the day, poked his head into the house that evening. Hearing no whining, he called out timidly, "Hello?"

"Hi, Dad!" Austin and Houston flew at him, wearing their new sneakers.

"We went to the shoe store today!" exclaimed Houston.

"I got sparkly sneakers," said Austin. "Look. They're purple. Just like Missy Piggle-Wiggle's dress."

"What?"

"And then we got ice cream for a treat," added Houston.

"Mr. Fester gave me the wrong cone," said Austin, "but Houston and I traded, so it was okay."

Mr. Forthright squeezed his eyes shut, waiting for the whining to begin. When it didn't, he slid all the way down onto the kitchen floor in a faint and had to be revived with smelling salts. Even so, his wife phoned Missy that night to thank her.

7

The Woe-Is-Me Cure

WAREFORD MONTPELIER'S FIRST bad day took
place shortly before summer vacation began. It started
the moment he woke up one morning. He rolled out of
bed and sleepily walked into the wall. He let out a yelp.
Huh, thought Wareford. *I got up on the wrong side of the
bed.* This had never happened to him before. Wareford
brushed his teeth and dressed for school. On his way to
breakfast, he tripped on the stairs and fell down the
last three steps.

"Wary?" called his father from the kitchen. "Are
you all right?"

Wareford was sitting on his bottom by an armchair.

"I guess so," he said. He rubbed his hip. Then he walked to the breakfast table, plopped down on his chair, and slipped off the other side. He landed on his bottom again.

"What is *wrong* with you?" asked Charlemagne. Charlemagne was Wary's sister. She was fourteen years old and embarrassed by everything Wary did, even if she was the only one there to see it.

"Charlemagne! Have a bit of sympathy for your brother," said Mrs. Montpelier. She helped her son back onto his chair.

"Well," said Wareford. "At least it's over now."

"What's over?" asked his father.

"My streak of bad luck. Three bad things happened. I walked into the wall, I fell down the stairs, and I fell out of my chair. That should be the end of the streak. Bad things happen in threes."

"Maybe," said his sister, "this was just the first of three *groups* of three bad things. Maybe six more bad things will happen to you today." Charlemagne drew comfort from the fact that since she was fourteen and Wary was ten, they went to different schools and rode different buses. She wouldn't be anywhere near Wary if six more embarrassingly bad things should happen to him.

"Charlemagne, for heaven's *sake!*" exclaimed her mother.

"Oh, I'm okay," said Wary confidently, and then he bit his tongue.

It began to bleed.

"Ew! Disgusting!" cried Charlemagne. She grabbed her backpack and ran out the front door.

Mr. and Mrs. Montpelier got Wary some ice and gauze. When the bleeding had stopped, he grabbed his own backpack. "Thee you after thcool," he lisped. He walked out the door more slowly than usual, eyes peeled for anything he might trip over. Ten minutes later, he reached the bus stop. He was the only one there. Three blocks away, his bus was turning a corner, heading for the next stop.

Wary slowly made his way home again. "I mithed the buth," he announced.

"Oh, dear," said his mother. "Well, don't worry. I'll drop you off on my way to work."

Before Wary even reached his classroom that day, he got locked in the boys' bathroom. He had stepped inside to examine his tongue in the mirror. When he was satisfied that the bleeding had truly stopped, he picked up his backpack and tugged at the handle of the door. He tugged and tugged and tugged. *Yikes!* he thought. *I'm locked in the bathroom.* This had never happened before, either.

"Hello?" he called.

Nothing.

"Hello? HELLO?!"

He put his ear to the door and listened, but because he had arrived at school late, the halls were quiet—everyone was already in class.

Wary tugged at the handle again. He tried pushing at the door, just in case he had forgotten how it worked. He shoved against it with all his might. Then he grabbed the handle and pulled with all his might.

More nothing.

Wary had opened his mouth to scream "SOME-BODY GET ME OUT OF HERE!" when he heard knocking on the other side of the door.

"Is somebody stuck in there?"

Wary recognized the voice of Mr. Samsonite, the maintenance man. He drooped with relief. "Yes! It's me, Wareford Montpelier. Get me out! I mean, please get me out!"

It took a crowbar, half an hour, and two people from the maintenance crew, but at last Wary was free. He should have been relieved, but all he could think about was what Charlemagne had said: that nine bad things might happen to him that day. He was up to only number six. Three more to go.

~~~~~~

When Wary returned from his long bad day at school, he slumped into Charlemagne's bedroom and let out a moan. "You were wrong."

Charlemagne crossed her arms and glared at him. "About what?"

"You said three groups of three bad things were going to happen to me today. That's nine. And I'm already up to number eleven."

Wary thought he saw his sister's face soften. "Really? Eleven bad things?" she said.

"Yes. After I bit my tongue, I missed the bus, got

locked in the bathroom, got thirty-eight percent on a surprise math quiz, got picked last for kickball, lost my hat, tripped over a tree root, and re-bit my tongue." Wary looked at his watch. "And it's only four o'clock."

"I'm sorry," said Charlemagne.

At bedtime that night, Mr. Montpelier sat next to his son and patted his arm while Wary again listed the bad things, which now numbered fourteen.

"It was just a rotten day," said his father.

His mother stepped into the room and handed him a chocolate candy. "Tomorrow is bound to be better," she added.

"How about if I read you a chapter of *Lassie*?" asked his father.

Wary looked listlessly at his parents while he unwrapped the chocolate. "Thanks," he said.

~~~~~

When Wary awoke the next morning, he found that he felt rather hopeful. He lay in his bed for a few moments, thinking about the previous day. Finally, he said aloud, "How could today be any worse?" He sat up slowly and swung his legs over the nonwall side of the bed.

He got dressed without incident.

He made his way to the doorway of the kitchen without incident.

And then Shady, the Montpeliers' cat, pounced on his feet from under the table, and Wary tripped, fell into Shady's water bowl, hit his head on a cabinet door as he stood up, fell down again, knocked his glasses to the floor, and closed his hand over a spider as he groped for the glasses.

"Aughhhhhhh!" he screamed.

Charlemagne regarded her brother with awe. "He's like all Three Stooges rolled into one," she said.

"How can this be happening?" asked Wary. He found his glasses, washed the hand that had touched the spider, and mopped up the spilled water. Then he felt the top of his head. "I'm bleeding," he announced. "Again."

"Gross!" exclaimed Charlemagne and fled from the house.

Mrs. Montpelier handed Wary a tissue. Then she tossed something into his lunch bag. "A little extra treat." She smiled at him.

Mr. Montpelier said, "Why don't I drive you to school today?"

"Thank you. That's a good idea," said Wary. "Because if I took the bus, I'd probably trip in the aisle, no one would want to sit with me, I'd get bus-sick—"

"You've never in your life gotten bus-sick, dear," said his mother.

"I've never fallen in a water bowl, either." Wary lowered himself cautiously onto his chair. "Also," he continued, "the bus would probably get a flat tire—"

"Well, you don't need to worry about those things, since I'm going to drive you," his father pointed out.

～～～

When Wary returned from school that afternoon, he found Charlemagne and her friend Desiree sitting side by side on the front steps.

"Here he is!" Charlemagne exclaimed. "Wary, how many bad things happened to you today?"

Wareford melted onto the bottom step and put his head in his hands. "Twelve. So far," he muttered. "And I'm counting the water bowl and the spider and the bleeding head as all one thing."

"See?" Charlemagne said to Desiree. "What did I tell you?"

Wareford was feeling too sorry for himself to care that his sister sounded proud of him. After a few moments, he realized that Desiree had leaned down and was staring at him.

"Is your nose bleeding?" she asked.

"A little. I fell onto Georgie Pepperpot's elbow."

There was silence, and finally Charlemagne said, "Wary, don't you want to go inside and put your things away?"

He sighed. "You'd better help me up the steps. I might fall."

Charlemagne didn't bother to point out that Wary could hold on to the railing. She took her brother gently by the elbow and guided him all the way into the kitchen. Desiree joined them, and the girls fixed Wary a snack. When he finished it, he sat where he was and did his homework, figuring it was best not to move around too much. He didn't leave his chair until bedtime.

~~~~~

The next morning, which was Saturday, Wary slept late and went downstairs in his pajamas. He spent two hours curled up on the couch under a blanket.

"Are you sick?" Charlemagne asked him.

"No," replied Wary, eyes downcast.

"Don't you want to play outside?" said his mother. "It's a beautiful day."

Wary ignored the question. "Are you going to the store this morning?" he asked.

"Yes. Why?"

"You'd better stock up on Band-Aids and first-aid cream." As his mother left the house, Wary called after her, "Drive carefully," but his voice was so weak, she didn't hear him.

~~~~~

It didn't take long for Charlemagne to tire of her brother's behavior.

"At first I thought he was cute," said Charlemagne, "but now he's just like, '*Wah-wah-wah*. Look at all the bad things that happen to me.'"

Mrs. Montpelier shook her head. "He barely leaves the house, and it's *summer vacation*."

"What should we do?" asked Mr. Montpelier.

Nobody knew. They had never encountered behavior like Wary's before.

At lunchtime that day, Georgie Pepperpot rang the Montpeliers' bell. "Let's go ride our bikes!" he said to Wary.

"I'd better not. I might fall off."

That afternoon, Rusty Goodenough stopped by. "Wary, come with me to watch the Little League game. Linden is playing."

"I'd better not. I might get hit in the head with a ball."

After Wary and Charlemagne had gone to bed that night, their parents sat on the front porch in the warm July air.

Mrs. Montpelier let out a sigh. "Isn't this wonderful?" she said. "A perfect summer evening. I love summer. Just think, a month from now we'll be at the beach. Two whole weeks at the shore."

Her husband cleared his throat. "Well . . ."

"Uh-oh. What?"

"I mentioned the beach to Wary this evening—you know, trying to give him something to look forward to—and what do you think he said? He said, 'The beach doesn't sound very safe, Dad. Maybe we shouldn't go. There could be a tidal wave. What if I get washed away by a tidal wave? Or I could get bitten by a shark or step on a broken seashell with my bare feet or stay out in the sun too long.'"

Mr. Montpelier turned to his wife. "Oh, dear," she said. But then she began to smile. "I think I know how to make him feel better. I'll point out how unlikely all these things are. The tidal wave, for instance. Do you think there has *ever* been a tidal wave at the Jersey Shore? I'll talk to him tomorrow. I'll let him know there's really nothing to be afraid of."

Wary's mother couldn't wait to present him with a few facts. The moment he got up the next morning, she said to him, "Wary, I understand you have some concerns about our vacation in Avalon. Do you know that I was doing some research about tidal waves"— (This was a lie. Wary's mother hadn't so much as googled "tidal waves.")—"and there has never, ever been a tidal wave at—"

Wary interrupted his mother. "Don't you always tell Charlemagne and me that there's a first time for everything?"

"Yes. . . ."

"For instance, falling in Shady's water bowl?"

"Well . . ."

"Since I'm a bad-luck magnet, I could easily attract the first tidal wave to New Jersey. And you don't want us to get swept away, do you?"

"Of course not, but . . . but . . ." Mrs. Montpelier couldn't even figure out how to finish her sentence.

Mr. Montpelier tried a different approach. "You know, Wary," he said that afternoon. They were in the garage. Wary had agreed to toss a ball with his father, but only if they played with a foam ball. Also, just in case he fell down, Wary had put on elbow pads, knee-pads, and a football helmet. "Some things can't be avoided," his father continued.

"What things can't be avoided?"

"The sun, for instance."

"That's why the beach isn't a good idea. It's also why we're playing catch in the garage."

Mr. Montpelier put his arm around Wary. "But you don't want to sit in the house all day when we go to Avalon, do you? That wouldn't be any fun."

"Oh, staying indoors wouldn't solve anything," said Wary. "The tidal wave could still get me."

Mr. Montpelier went inside and found his wife. "We have a distinct problem," he whispered to her.

~~~~~~

Across Little Spring Valley, the yard at Missy Piggle-Wiggle's was a busy place. Fourteen children, many of them friends of Wary's, were jumping rope, climbing trees, and looking for treasure. Three children had dressed themselves in clothes from Missy's costume box and were playing *Rock Band*. Tulip Goodenough and Samantha Tickle were sitting in the grass by a garden weaving daisy chains.

Melody sat alone on the front porch, watching Tulip and Samantha. She had asked if she could join them, and Samantha had replied, "Why? So you can tell us how they make daisy chains in Utopia? Maybe our way is better."

So now Melody sat on the top step, chin in her hands. She didn't even look at Lester when he settled down beside her. After a long time, he placed one front hoof on her hand and patted her gently. Even though this felt like being patted by a coconut, Melody offered him a small smile.

A few minutes later, Missy joined them on the porch. She sat on the swing, and as she swayed back and forth, her lavender dress shimmered and wafted around her legs. She looked from Melody and Lester to Tulip and Samantha, but all she said was, "I haven't seen Wareford Montpelier in quite some time. Is his family away on vacation?"

"I don't think so," replied Melody.

From the flower garden, Tulip called, "He doesn't leave his house anymore! Rusty told me so."

Samantha nudged her friend and said in a whisper loud enough for everyone on the porch to hear, "Don't say that! Melody will blame it on Little Spring Valley."

Missy considered what she had heard. Her eyes narrowed slightly, and you would have had to look into them very closely to see that they were glittering. At the same time, for the briefest moment, her hair sprang up as if electrified. Then it settled back onto her shoulders, and she said comfortably, "Why isn't Wary leaving his house?"

"Afraid," said Samantha.

"Afraid of what?" Melody dared to ask.

"Everything," said Tulip.

Missy left the porch and climbed the stairs to her bedroom. Today the house had floated all the rugs up to the ceilings, so Missy clumped along noisily on the bare floors, sending up a little puff of dust with each step. She waved to Serena, who was wrestling with a radiator in Mrs. Piggle-Wiggle's bedroom, and then she went into her own room, unlocked the potion cabinet, and surveyed the bottles and jars and packets inside. She saw that three had worked their way to the front of the shelves: the Don't-Want-to-Try Cure, the I-Can't Cure, and a general Fear-All Cure.

"Thank you," Missy said to the cabinet. "I don't know yet if I'll need any of you, but my fingertips are telling me I'll be getting a phone call very soon."

The call came shortly after seven that evening. Wareford's father was on the other end of the line. "We've never experienced anything like this!" he exclaimed to Missy. "Not with Charlemagne, and not with Wary until—"

"Until he had a bad day?" suggested Missy.

"Exactly. But it wasn't just one day. He had a streak of bad luck. It went on for quite a while."

"It's natural to want to coddle a child during a time like that."

Wary's father frowned at the phone. "We didn't exactly *coddle* him," he said, even as he thought about chocolate candies and rides to school and the mornings Wary was allowed to spend lying on the couch. How on earth did Missy Piggle-Wiggle know what had gone on during the past few weeks?

"In any case, Wareford needs to feel safe again," said Missy.

"Yes," replied Mr. Montpelier. "And he needs to feel in control again."

"Exactly. I wonder if you could spare Wary for a day or so. Could he come stay with me at the upside-down house?"

Mr. Montpelier pretended to think this over. "Goodness," he said at last. "Part with Wareford for several *days*? I don't know. I'll have to check with my wife. I'll get back to you later this evening."

Wareford's father was aware that Missy was as magical as her great-aunt, so he hoped she couldn't somehow see that as soon as he clicked off the phone, he picked up Shady and danced her around the kitchen, then poked his head out the back door and shouted, "Yahoo!" into the twilight. After that, he ran through the house to the living room. "Dear! Dear!" he called to his wife with great excitement. Then he lowered his voice. "Where's Wary?"

"Upstairs. Still finishing his dinner in bed. He's having a particularly difficult day, poor lamb."

"Guess what Missy said," Mr. Montpelier whispered. He told his wife that they were going to have a little break from Wareford.

"I wonder what Missy plans to do with him?" said Mrs. Montpelier, frowning. "I hope it isn't too drastic. Wary is more nervous every day."

"All I know is that he's going to come home cured."

It was Wary's mother who called Missy back later. "What should we pack for him?" she asked. "Is there a fee involved? Can we bring him tonight?"

"First thing tomorrow morning will be fine," Missy said crisply. "I need to get his room ready."

~~~~~~

In truth, all it took was a snap of Missy's fingers to transform the guest room into a sanctuary for Wareford

Montpelier. She stood at the door, raised her hand, and snap! A small green tornado whisked itself into shape and whirled through the room, sweeping away the bed with its dust ruffle and spread, the dresser with its cheerful rose-colored knobs, the table with its stack of storybooks, and the child-size desk and chair. Left in its wake was the perfect environment in which to put into effect the Woe-Is-Me Cure.

Missy looked at the room with satisfaction and then hurried downstairs. "Lester, Penelope, Wag, Lightfoot," she said. "We're going to have company for a couple of days. I expect you to be on your best behavior."

Lester bowed. Penelope cocked her head and squawked, "Just what I was hoping for—more people in the house!" Wag wagged his tail. Lightfoot turned her back and edged out of the room.

"House?" said Missy. "Will you behave, too? We have work to do."

The house dumped all the rugs back down to the floors.

"Thank you," said Missy.

The next morning, Harold stopped at the upside-down house on his way to work to check on the progress of the repairs. He and Missy were chatting with Serena, who was saying, "I think that at last we're nearly done," when the Montpeliers arrived. The entire family had come to see Wary off. Mr. and Mrs. Montpelier sprang out of the front seat. Charlemagne tried to open her door, found it locked, and, in her excitement, thrust herself through the open window. "Come on, Wary!" she called to her brother. She reached back through the window and yanked at his wrist.

Wary slowly unbuckled his seat belt. Then he unlocked the door, opened it cautiously, and looked up and down the sidewalk to make sure he wouldn't get run over by a tricycle or a scooter.

Meanwhile, Mrs. Montpelier had opened the trunk, removed Wary's suitcase, and carried it across the yard. She waited while her son crept along the walk to Missy's porch. "Remember your manners," she said, stooping to Wary's level and resting her hand on his cheek. Then she pulled him close for a hug.

"Thank you so much, Missy," said her husband, and he hugged Wary, too, before dashing back to the car.

"Yes, thank you!" added Charlemagne.

The Montpeliers sped off down the street.

Harold frowned after them. "They practically left tire marks on the road," he whispered to Missy.

"I'm afraid this is a rather extreme case."

"An extreme case of what?"

"Woe-Is-Me Syndrome."

"Hmm."

Missy looked at Wary, who was sitting at the very edge of a porch chair in case he needed to make a quick getaway from a bee. "I understand you've been having a bit of a hard time," she said to him gently.

Wary nodded, and tears filled his eyes. "Bad things just keep happening to me. One after another."

"Well, I have the perfect solution for you." Missy held out her hand. "Come with me. I'll show you to the guest room."

Wary had stayed in the guest room at his grand-father's house many times. There was a bed in it with four tall posts and a pale-blue canopy draped across the top. There was a dresser in which he could put his clothes, but the bottom drawer of the dresser was full of things that had belonged to his mother when she was a little girl. Wary liked to take them out and examine them: a seashell, a pin from the Girl Scouts, photos, awards. Plus there was a cupboard full of toys and games that his grandfather had bought brand-new, just for Wary and Charlemagne.

So you can imagine Wary's surprise when Missy opened the door to the guest room at the upside-down house and he saw nothing but padding. The floor, the walls, and even the ceiling were covered with what looked like mattresses. The windows were edged with giant cotton balls, and the panes of glass had been removed and replaced with screens.

Wary was speechless. He glanced behind him into the hall where Missy stood, smiling. Next to her was Lester, the polite pig who had helpfully carried Wary's suitcase up the stairs, and next to *him* was Harold Spectacle from the bookstore, wearing an astonished expression. The expression was mirrored on Serena's face when she passed by the guest room.

"Did you want me to do some repairs in here, too?" she asked just as Wary said, "This is the guest room?" He thought Missy must have mistakenly opened the door to a storage room.

Missy said, "No, thank you," to Serena, and, "Yes, it's all yours," to Wareford.

"But where do I sleep?" asked Wary.

"Why, right there on the floor. It's nice and soft and cushiony. Impossible for you to get hurt."

"What am I supposed to do in here?"

"What do you mean?"

"Well . . ." Wary didn't want to be an impolite guest. "Could I have a TV?"

"Heavens, no. You might run into it. Or it might topple over on you."

Wary nodded thoughtfully. "That's true. Then how about a pad of paper and a pencil?"

"A *pencil?* Out of the question. You could jab yourself with it," said Missy. "Maybe I'll give you a crayon. Just don't accidentally swallow it."

Wary stepped into the room and stood on the padding. He turned around and around. "Should I take off my shoes?"

"Good idea. I see that yours have laces. Laces can be very dangerous indeed." Missy held out her hand for the sneakers.

"Oh, I know all about laces," said Wary. "I've already

tripped over them twice. Mom wouldn't let me get new shoes, though."

Enough dilly-dallying, thought Missy. She blinked her eyes. She blinked them four times, but she did it so fast that all anyone saw was one blink—and then Penelope screeched from her perch on the banister, "It's nine thirty, Harold Spectacle!"

Harold snapped to attention. "Time for me to get to the store," he exclaimed.

"Time for me to get back to work," said Serena.

Wary turned warily around in his new room.

~~~~~~

Wareford's first day at Missy's seemed a bit long, but he didn't want to be rude and complain. For a while, he simply sat on the padded floor. When he heard shouts from outside, he got to his feet and bounced his way across the padding to the window, grateful not to have to worry about tripping over anything. He leaned on the cotton balls and looked at the yard below. He saw Rusty and Tulip teaching Veronica Cupcake how to hit a softball. After two misses, her bat connected with the ball—*thwack!*—and the ball soared across the yard.

"Home run!" shouted Tulip.

In his room, Wary ducked and plopped down on the mattress. "That was close," he said to Wag, who was peeking at him from the hallway. But soon, because there was absolutely nothing else to do, Wary found himself looking out the window again. This time he saw Veronica hit a ball, toss her bat to the ground, trip over it, and skin her knee.

"Ow!" she cried. But then she brightened. "Hey, now Missy will give me a Band-Aid."

"Hmm," said Wary from his padded room.

Down below, Linden Pettigrew yanked Missy's garden hose around to a pot of begonias, turned the water on, and managed to spray himself from head to toe before unsticking the nozzle. "Ha!" he hooted. "That's the third time I've done that this week. Oh, well."

"Interesting," murmured Wareford.

An hour passed, and then another.

"Missy?" called Wary.

Missy appeared instantly.

"I thought you were outside," said Wary, who had just seen her handing a volleyball to Tulip.

"Hmm. Well, was there something you wanted?"

Wary peered over Missy's shoulder. How had she climbed the stairs so quickly—and so quietly? "I was wondering about the paper and . . . crayon." Wary hadn't used a crayon in three years.

"Certainly," said Missy, and from nowhere a red satchel appeared on her shoulder. She opened it and produced a blue crayon and several sheets of paper. "Here you go. Now I'd better see about some lunch for you."

In the guest room of the upside-down house, Wary sat on the floor and tried to draw a picture. Every time he pressed the crayon to a piece of paper, the paper sank into the mattress, forming a soft crater.

Downstairs in the kitchen, Missy looked through her cupboards, which were nearly bare. *I really must search for the silver key*, she thought. *But not today. Today I must concentrate on Wareford.* She set out a tray, and on it she placed a plastic cup of applesauce, a plastic cup of cold soup, and a paper plate holding a piece of buttered bread. Next to the plate, she placed a plastic spoon. Nothing breakable, nothing sharp, and nothing Wary could choke on or burn his tongue with.

"Lunchtime!" announced Missy. She stood outside

Wary's room and looked in at a sea of crumpled papers, each decorated by a few faint blue marks.

"Oh, good," replied Wareford, brushing aside the papers.

Missy left the tray in the hall and carried the food to her guest. She set the plate and cups on the floor and handed Wary the spoon.

"Um . . ." said Wary.

"Oh, of course. You'll need something to eat on."

Missy hurried away and returned with a puffy pillow. "Just set this on your lap and use it like a table."

"Thank you," said Wary politely. "This is all very"— he paused—"very soft."

"And very safe."

~~~~~

At bedtime that evening, Missy brought several blankets and another pillow into the guest room. She arranged them in the middle of the floor. "Sleep well," she said.

Harold Spectacle had arrived for another game of Scrabble with Missy and Lester, and he watched from the doorway. He was wearing a red-and-green striped vest and dark-green pants that billowed out from his waist and seemed to have many, many pockets. A watch on a chain looped from one pocket to another. Wary wondered what was in the others.

"If you don't mind my asking," said Harold, "why is Wareford sleeping in the middle of the room? Wouldn't a corner be cozier?"

"He has a habit of waking up and walking into walls," replied Missy.

"It's not exactly a habit," said Wary. "I only did that once."

"You can't be too careful, though."

"I suppose not."

Harold suddenly looked as though he felt sorry for Wary. "Would you like me to read to you for a while?" he asked.

"Yes, please," replied Wary, who was wondering how he was going to sleep in this strange room with no curtains at the window and the moon shining brightly.

Harold found a copy of *The Twenty-One Balloons* and carried it into the guest room.

"Wait!" cried Missy. She held up her hands. "Sit out here in the hall. It's much safer for Wary."

"But that's a paperback book," said Wary.

"Still," replied Missy.

So Harold sat in the doorway of Wary's room and began the story about the incredible adventure of Professor Sherman.

"A wise choice," Missy whispered to Harold.

"Thank you."

~~~~~

Somehow Wary managed to fall asleep in his padded, protected room at the upside-down house. The next morning, he wobbled across the mattresses to the door and flung it open, ready to call good morning to Missy. To his surprise, he found her standing in the hallway. She was holding a breakfast tray with an array of very soft foods.

"Hello, Wary," she said. "I have a nice runny egg for you and some yogurt and another cup of applesauce."

"Thank you," Wary replied. "But, before I eat, could we talk?"

"Of course." Missy's eyes glittered as she left the tray in the hall and joined Wary on the floor. "What would you like to talk about?"

"Me." Wary thought for a moment. "And Professor Sherman."

"Professor Sherman from the book?"

"Yes. I was thinking about how brave he was. And about how he set out to do one thing, and then got caught up in something else and had a wonderful adventure in Krakatoa."

"That's the magic of books," said Missy. "You can read about all sorts of things."

"But I kind of miss actually *doing* things. Nothing is ever going to happen to me if I just lie around my house."

"Then how are you going to avoid tripping and falling and—"

"And getting whacked with a softball and stepping on a seashell? I guess I can't. Not if I want to play outdoors with my friends and go on vacation with my family."

"Or fly to Krakatoa," said Missy.

Wareford nodded. "Anyway, I'm in charge of me, and I can decide whether I want to laugh or cry when I spray myself with the garden hose. Do you understand what I mean?"

"Perfectly."

Wary waded across the padding to the window and looked outside. "Linden and Beaufort are already here," he said.

"Do you want to join them?" asked Missy.

Wary thought about another day of mattresses and applesauce. "Yes," he said, "but first I want to talk to my parents."

Missy handed Wary the phone, and he called his family and told them he was coming home.

8

Girls' Day

ON A MIDSUMMER day that felt more like October than August, Missy Piggle-Wiggle bustled around the farmyard behind the upside-down house. Penelope swooped after her. "Chilly!" she squawked.

"It won't last," said Missy. She turned to Warren and Evelyn's goslings, who had grown so fast that they were already as big as their parents. "Here you go," she said. "Lunchtime." She scattered corn across the ground for them. When she dropped the bucket back in the corn bin, she heard a *clunk*. The bin was now empty.

"Tsk, tsk," tutted Penelope. "Down to nothing. What are you going to do?"

"Forge ahead," Missy replied.

"Hello!" called a chorus of voices.

Running across the yard came Honoriah and Petulance Freeforall, Tulip Goodenough, and Samantha Tickle. They were wearing sweatshirts and rubbing their hands together.

"It's freezing!" cried Petulance.

"Tell her why we're here," Samantha whispered to Tulip.

"You're here for a particular reason?" asked Missy.

"Yes." Tulip nodded her head. "We have a problem."

"Aha," said Missy, her fingertips tingling.

"We have a *severe* problem," said Honoriah.

"Don't exaggerate," said Tulip.

"I'm not exaggerating!"

The girls were jumping up and down.

"We need help!"

"It's dire!"

"Goodness, let's go inside," said Missy, and she led her guests into the kitchen of the upside-down house, where they crowded around the table.

"Lester," said Missy, "I think we have just enough

powder left to make six mugs of hot chocolate. Don't we?"

Lester looked uncomfortable, but then he checked the hot chocolate tin, nodded at Missy, and reached for the kettle, which was already boiling.

"Okay," Missy said to the girls. "What seems to be the trouble?"

There was a pause followed by an eruption of voices that tumbled over one another.

"It's Melody!"

"She's driving us crazy."

"We can't talk to her anymore."

"She's all, 'In Utopia we did it this way' and 'Utopia is so great' and 'My friends in Utopia were perfect.'"

"She's a pain in my brain."

Missy accepted a warm mug from Lester. "Thank you," she said. She took a sip of hot chocolate. Then she turned to the girls. "I think you need to talk to Melody."

"*Talk* to her?!"

"We can't."

"We tried."

"It didn't help."

"Do you *want* to patch things up with Melody?" asked Missy.

"Yes," said Samantha.

"Why?"

Samantha looked surprised. "Because she's our friend."

"All right, then," said Missy. "That's a good starting place. Now the next step is to think about how you're going to patch things up."

"How *we're* going to patch things up?" repeated Tulip. "We thought *you* were going to do that. We thought you would cure Melody."

"With your magic," added Petulance.

"Like you cured us," said Honoriah.

"Not everything can be fixed with magic," replied Missy Piggle-Wiggle.

"Why not? Magic is magic," said Samantha.

Missy drew herself up tall and recalled her days teaching at the Magic Institute for Children. "Magic," she said primly, "is different for everyone. We all have magic in us. Some of us have a lot of magic; some have a little. Everyone's magic is different. I am very good with cures, that's true, but I have my limits. For instance, I can't just wave my hand and"—Missy thought about the empty corn bin and the empty chocolate tin and the enormous bill she was about to get from Serena Clutter—"make dollar bills appear in my pocketbook. Some things must be worked for."

"Well, that is not what I wanted to hear," said Tulip crossly.

Honoriah frowned. "We thought you could do anything."

"Anyone can do anything," said Missy. "You need to find the proper way to go about whatever it is you want to do."

"Will you help us?" asked Petulance.

"Of course. Now, have you ever heard of Girls' Day?"

Honoriah, Petulance, Tulip, and Samantha shook their heads.

Missy hadn't heard of Girls' Day, either, since she had just that very second made it up.

"Is it a special day for girls only?" asked Honoriah.

"Why, yes it is," replied Missy.

"Here at your house?" asked Samantha.

"All right."

"Are there special activities?" asked Tulip.

"Yes."

"Like art projects and making brownies and maybe having a dress-up picnic?" asked Samantha.

"Absolutely," said Missy. "And who do you think should be invited to Girls' Day?"

"Well, all of us," answered Petulance. "And you."

"And the girl animals," said Tulip. "Lightfoot and Penelope."

"Anyone else?" asked Missy.

"Melody?" said Honoriah in a small voice.

"I think that would be splendid," said Missy. "And of course, you can invite other girls as well. It's up to you."

"But Girls' Day," said Samantha slowly, "will be a way for us to show Melody how much we like her?"

"And that we truly want to be her friends?" added Petulance.

"Yes," said Missy. "That's important, because she still misses her old home and her old friends and her old life. It can be hard to be the new kid. But Melody does want to be friends with you."

"She's always—" Tulip began to protest.

"Sometimes you have to make an extra effort,"

Missy continued. "Beyond whatever you've already done." Missy produced a pad of paper and a pencil from somewhere the girls couldn't quite see, even though Honoriah peeped under the table and Samantha tried to peek up Missy's sleeves. "All right. Let's start planning," said Missy. "Penelope, Lightfoot, why don't you join us?"

Penelope swooped into the kitchen from her perch by the front door, where she liked to watch for visitors to the upside-down house. Lightfoot, however, who was napping in the hallway, only opened one eye before going back to sleep.

"Let's talk about food!" squawked Penelope.

But Tulip said, "I don't want the boys to feel bad about Girls' Day. Especially you, Lester."

Lester, who was seated at one end of the table with a mug of coffee now that he'd finished his hot chocolate, dipped his bristly head and waved one hoof to let everyone know he wasn't offended.

"Still," Tulip continued, "I think the boys should be allowed to come over at the end of the day."

"Good idea," agreed Missy.

~~~~~

The girls planned activities and wrote out a menu for the Girls' Day picnic. They made an invitation for Melody. "We'll call up everyone else who's invited," said Honoriah, "but Melody gets a special invitation."

The girls took it to her personally at the end of the day after they had called good-bye to Missy and Lester. They hurried up the street and turned in at Melody's gate, whispering and giggling all the way to her porch.

"Should we ring the bell, leave the invitation, and hide?"

"No, put it in the mailbox."

"No, give it to her in person!"

In the end they didn't have a choice, because Melody heard the whispering and giggling and opened the door while they were still standing on her porch, holding the invitation.

"Hi!" said Melody. She felt surprised and just slightly suspicious, since her friends hadn't been to her house in quite some time. And hadn't spoken to her in almost as long.

Samantha, who was holding the envelope, stopped giggling and stood on one foot, scratching the back of her ankle with the other foot. She glanced at her friends, then thrust the invitation at Melody and said, "This is for you."

"What is it?"

"Open it."

Melody stepped all the way out onto the porch, letting the screen door swing shut behind her. She slit the envelope with her thumb and drew out a sheet of pink paper. This is what she saw:

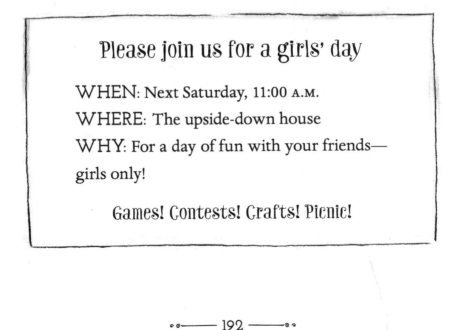

Please join us for a girls' day

WHEN: Next Saturday, 11:00 A.M.

WHERE: The upside-down house

WHY: For a day of fun with your friends—girls only!

Games! Contests! Crafts! Picnic!

"And you're our special guest," said Petulance.

"Really? Me?" said Melody in a small voice. "Thank you."

~~~~~

When Melody woke up on Girls' Day, she found a foggy, soggy morning, but she didn't care. She put on a yellow blouse and a pair of flowered shorts and tied a striped ribbon around her ponytail. At exactly 10:55 a.m., she left her house, turned right at the end of her walk, and continued down the lane to Missy's house. She felt that walking to the special party for girls all by herself was just a bit lonely. In Utopia, she would have walked to a party for girls with Pollyanna and Ashley-Sarah.

But Little Spring Valley was not Utopia.

Still, Melody put a smile on her face as she approached the porch of the upside-down house. From inside, she heard Penelope cry, "Melody Flowers is here!"

Moments later, the door was thrust open by Tulip. Crowded behind her were the Freeforall twins, Samantha Tickle, Veronica Cupcake, Heavenly Earwig, Tallulah Treadupon, Caramel Dolittle, and Austin Forthright.

"Surprise!" shouted Veronica.

Samantha nudged Veronica. "It isn't actually a surprise."

"I know, but I thought it would be fun to shout 'Surprise!' and it was."

"Welcome to Girls' Day," said Missy. "House decorated the hallway for you."

Brightly colored balloons rolled gently over the rugs. Crepe paper streamers crisscrossed the floor. A banner was stretched across the doorway to the parlor. Melody had to stand on her head in order to read it. It said WELCOME TO GIRLS' DAY!

"Everything is beautiful," said Melody softly.

"Now," said Missy, "the first thing we do on Girls' Day is hold a costume contest."

The girls dove for the costume box in the parlor.

"I'm going to be a mermaid!" cried Veronica.

"I'm going to be a Martian," said Heavenly.

Melody watched as the girls began claiming hats and wands and coats and false noses from the box.

"What are you going to be, Melody?" asked Missy.

"I—Maybe a parrot."

"Hurry up, then."

Melody looked at her friends, who were already wriggling into their costumes. She was sure nothing would be left in the box. But when she peered into it, she saw that it was still full and that, even better, a pile of orange-and-green feathers lay on the very top.

"Parrot wings!" she exclaimed. She had never seen parrot wings in the box before.

"Are there prizes?" Veronica asked a few minutes later when the girls were admiring their finished costumes.

"The prize," Missy replied, "is that it's time to look for pirate treasure."

"But it's raining!" exclaimed Caramel.

"That's why we're going on an indoor treasure hunt."

The girls spent the next hour searching the upside-down house. Melody found a very old toy truck under a chair. Veronica found a nickel and gave it to Missy to put in her purse. Austin found two marbles.

"We all found something," said Tallulah later. "Every single one of us. This must be our good-luck day."

It was too wet to hold the picnic outside, so the Girls' Day picnic took place in the parlor. It started on the floor, and then the guests, who were still wearing their costumes, and the food and the picnic blanket slowly rose toward the ceiling. Later, when Petulance was opening a floating box of cookies, Melody offered her a smile. Petulance smiled back.

"Thank you for inviting me to Girls' Day," said Melody.

Missy reached up to steady herself on the ceiling. "Your friends planned it for you. They wanted to do something special."

Melody nodded. "I know I've been talking about Utopia a lot, but guess what? There are a lot of things here in Little Spring Valley that Utopia doesn't have. Like an upside-down house. And a pig that can read and make coffee. And magic. And, of course, you and all my new friends."

Tulip beamed, but Missy said, "It isn't a contest between Utopia and Little Spring Valley, though. Both places have wonderful things and wonderful people. You can miss Utopia, Melody, but still appreciate what you have here. There's room for both."

Lightfoot crawled out from under a chair then and curled up in Melody's lap. She began to purr loudly.

"Hmm," said Missy.

"What?" asked Melody.

"Lightfoot really likes you. I don't think I've seen her this happy since before my aunt left."

Melody smiled, and Lightfoot rolled onto her back and stuck her feet in the air.

~~~~~

At three that afternoon, the girls, who were lying on the floor in the parlor while Missy read to them, heard a tentative knock on the front door, and Penelope screeched, "Linden Pettigrew and Rusty Goodenough are here!"

Lester opened the door and Linden said, "Is it okay for the boys to come in now?"

"Absolutely," said Missy.

Lester left the door standing open, and soon other boys began to trickle inside: Frankfort Freeforall, Houston Forthright, Einstein J. Treadupon. They joined the girls and listened to Missy read from *The Wind in the Willows*. Later, when dinnertime was drawing near and rumbling stomachs sent the children back to their homes, Melody helped Missy tidy the upside-down house. Before she left, she hugged Missy and said, "I had a talk with Lightfoot about being homesick. We both feel better now, and I didn't even need any magic."

9

The Silver Key

"WELL, THAT'S THAT," said Missy Piggle-Wiggle. She stood in the parlor of the upside-down house, her arms crossed, and regarded Lester, Wag, Lightfoot, and Penelope. The repairs on the house were completed and paid for, and the house was as right as rain again. But inside Missy's wallet was the recipe for the Grocery-Store-Tantrum potion . . . and nothing more.

Missy leafed again through the little stack of mail that had just been delivered and that she had set on a right-side-up table next to an upside-down chair. "Still no word from Auntie, and I can't wait a moment longer. We are completely out of money."

Penelope blinked her parrot eyes and flapped her wings. "It's a disaster! A catastrophe!" She swooped back and forth across the room until she crashed into a lamp, which Lester caught neatly between his front hooves and returned to its spot on a table.

Most people in this situation would have been as panicked as Penelope, but Missy lowered herself calmly onto the floor, crossed her legs, and put her chin in her hands to think. Lightfoot crawled into her lap, Wag sat next to her and offered his paw, and Lester smiled peacefully at her from his spot on the sofa.

"What about parrot food?" squawked Penelope. "Have we run out of parrot food?"

Lester frowned and put one hoof to his lips, shushing her.

Suddenly Missy clapped her hands together—once, smartly—and said, "Time to search for the silver key. And time to phone Harold."

~~~~~

At A to Z Books on Juniper Street, Harold Spectacle was talking with Melody, Samantha, Honoriah, Petulance, and Tulip. They were crowded around the checkout counter in great excitement. Melody's hair was flying out of its ponytails, Samantha was jumping up and down so hard that her socks had pooled around her ankles, and Honoriah, Petulance, and Tulip were giggling.

"We want to start a book club," Melody was saying. "Could we have our meetings here at the store?"

Before Harold could answer, Petulance stopped giggling long enough to say, "Can you give us a reading list?"

"Can we eat in the store?" asked Tulip. "We might want snacks."

Harold was about to say yes to all three requests when he was interrupted by a loud mooing. "Ah, the phone. Just let me answer that." Harold picked up the phone, and the mooing stopped. "A to Z Books," he said.

"Harold," said Missy, a formal tone to her voice, "the time has come to search for the silver key."

"I thought it might have," replied Harold. He adjusted his top hat, which was slipping over his forehead. "Would you like me to join you?"

"I would."

"Tonight?"

"Tonight."

And that was how the search for the silver key began.

~~~~~

"The problem is," said Missy as she ushered Harold into the upside-down house that evening, "I don't know a thing about the key, including how it will help me with money."

"You've never heard of the silver key before?" asked Harold. He was perched on the dusty underneath-side of a couch that the house had turned upside-down.

"Not until Auntie mentioned it in one of her letters."

"Hmm." Harold twisted the tails of his tuxedo jacket through his fingers. "Well, I suppose we can assume that if the key is meant to help you when you run out of money, then it will lead you to money."

"Yes, of course," said Missy.

"The question is—how?"

"Exactly," said Missy. She didn't want to complain, since it was nice to have a friend she could discuss things with, but really, Harold's reasoning was rather plodding.

"The most likely possibility is that the key will

unlock a trunk full of pirate treasure from your great-uncle. Just think, the lid will open with a *creeeeeeak*, and before we've raised it all the way, gold coins will start to spill out in a shimmering cascade." Harold gazed dreamily into the distance. "Under all the coins will be jewels—emeralds and diamonds and sapphires. Oh, and gold crowns studded with rubies!"

"I'm not sure it will be like pirate treasure in cartoons," said Missy. "I'm not even sure it will be pirate treasure."

"Why not?" said Harold. He jumped to his feet. "Let's go to the attic!"

Missy and Harold hurried up two flights of stairs. Lester followed them. Wag followed Lester, Lightfoot followed Wag, and Penelope flapped along behind Lightfoot.

Missy opened the door to the newly finished attic.

"Serena and her team did a wonderful job," said Harold, looking from the brand-new wall to the brand-new shelves to the brand-new cabinets, but he sounded disappointed.

"What's the matter?" asked Missy.

"It's just that, well, it's so *neat* up here now. I was

expecting more of a mess. Like most attics. Plus, I don't see a single pirate trunk."

"There's still plenty to explore. And anyway, the first thing we have to do is find the key. Then we can figure out what it opens."

"True," said Harold. He looked admiringly at Missy.

Missy, Harold, and Lester opened the cabinets and began to search them. Wag sniffed every inch of the floor with her snuffly nose. Penelope sat on a shelf and shouted out orders. "Don't forget to look in the corners! Open every box, *every* box!"

Lightfoot curled up on an old coat and fell asleep.

Lester found a box of clothes and tried them on. He stood in front of a mirror and regarded himself in a top hat and tux.

"Why, he looks just like me," commented Harold.

"Well . . ." said Missy. She felt that there was a vast difference between Harold and a pig, but she had to admit that Lester looked rather dapper.

Penelope bounced up and down on the shelf. "You're wasting time! Get a move on! Lightfoot, look alive!"

Missy opened cartons containing old linens and old dishes. She found a box of hats that she set aside to add to the dress-up box. Harold found a carton of children's books with fading covers that Missy also decided to take downstairs.

They opened doors and drawers and pawed through boxes until finally Harold sat down and scratched his head. "Nothing," he said. He paused. "I've just thought of something. Maybe there's a book called *The Silver Key*! Maybe that's what we're supposed to search for."

"Hurry!" screeched Penelope.

Harold lovingly read the title of each book in the box, but then he sighed. "Nope. Nothing called *The Silver Key*. And nothing about a key or a lock or a treasure."

"But that was a good idea," said Missy. "It reminds me that we must think creatively."

"We must think outside the box," added Harold.

Lester nodded and tapped his forehead with his hoof.

Lightfoot yawned.

"All right. Start over, everyone," said Missy.

Harold returned to the box of books and flipped

through each one. "No secret compartments," he said. "No clues hidden between the pages."

Missy examined the hats again, although she couldn't imagine what she might find. She shook out the linens. Lester shook out the clothes.

"Nothing," said Missy.

"There are plenty more cartons to look through," said Harold.

"Keep going!" called Penelope just as Wag gave up sniffing and curled up next to Lightfoot.

Missy, Harold, and Lester searched for another hour. They found more clothes and books. They found a large box that contained . . . "Auntie's wedding gown!" exclaimed Missy. They found lamp shades and pans and boring-looking receipts and rolled-up rugs.

They also found a locked toolbox, a table with a locked drawer, and a red box, highly polished and decorated with tiny silver flowers, that was locked and that rattled when they shook it.

"At least," said Missy, "when we do find the key, we have three locks to try it in."

Lester tugged at Missy's sleeve and pantomimed

pouring something into a cup and raising the cup to his bristly pig lips.

"Absolutely," agreed Missy. "Time to break for tea."

"Ten minutes," muttered Penelope.

"I think twenty will be fine," replied Missy crisply.

She and Harold and Lester went back downstairs, Harold clickety-clacking along with the cane he didn't need. In the kitchen, Lester set the kettle on the old black stove and waited for the water to boil.

Penelope swooped into the room behind them and squawked, "A lost cause!"

Missy shook her head. "It is not a lost cause."

Harold once again looked at her admiringly. Some people, he thought, would have given up by now. "It's nowhere to be found," they might have said, or "I think we're on a wild-goose chase." But not Missy.

"I have a feeling," she added, "that we'll find it before the night is out."

Fortified with tea, Missy and her friends returned to the attic. They stepped over the sleeping Lightfoot and Wag.

"Remember to be creative," said Missy.

Harold pried up a loose floorboard that Serena and her team had missed. Underneath was just what you'd expect to find: dust. Lester felt around for secret compartments and hidden drawers. Missy found some old dried-up potions belonging to Mrs. Piggle-Wiggle, and Harold found some scarves and eye patches and other discarded pirate clothing.

"Maybe," said Missy, who now looked rather grimy, "the silver key is what we heard rattling around in the red box."

"Smash it!" cried Penelope.

"Smash the box?" exclaimed Missy. "For heaven's sake, settle down, Penelope."

In the end, it was Lester who located the silver key. He had dragged a chair across the floor to the attic doorway, the one doorway in the entire house that wasn't upside-down, stood on the chair on tippy-hooves, and felt around—and there on the ledge above the door was a key.

A large silver key, like something that would open a giant's diary.

Lester jumped to the ground and in his excitement

began to oink. He held out the key and oinked and grunted and snurfled.

"The key!" cried Missy.

"We're saved!" cried Penelope.

"It wasn't actually hidden at all," said Harold.

"But we almost didn't find it," replied Missy. "Auntie is very clever. It was hiding in plain sight."

Missy, Harold, Lester, and Penelope gazed at the key shining on Lester's outstretched hooves.

"It's bigger than I thought it would be," said Harold. "And it's so shiny."

"It's beautiful," whispered Missy. She took it from Lester and turned it around and around. Then she rested it on her palm. It was the heaviest key she had ever held. "Now the question is, of course, what does it open?"

"We know three locks we can try it in," Harold reminded her.

They started with the toolbox but saw immediately that the key was too big.

"Toadstools!" screeched Penelope and began hopping up and down on Missy's shoulder.

"Try the table next," suggested Harold.

Missy sat on the floor in front of the table and carefully stuck the key in the lock. It fit, just barely, but it wouldn't turn.

"Let me try," said Harold. He twisted the key from side to side, but the only thing that happened was that his wrist began to ache. He pulled the key out. "I hope it opens the red box."

Missy detected a note of desperation in his voice.

"I want to do it!" squawked Penelope. She jumped to the floor, and Harold placed the key in her left claw. She eyed the key, then the lock. "Won't work!" she announced.

"Please try it anyway," said Missy.

Penelope balanced on her right leg while Missy held the box steady.

Sure enough, the key was too big.

"Told you so!" cried Penelope.

"What do you suppose is rattling around in there?" asked Harold.

"I don't know, but we aren't going to smash the box," said Missy.

She sat on the floor with a thump. Penelope paced

back and forth in front of her. "What a conundrum," she said.

Lester frowned.

"It means enigma," said Harold. "Mystery, riddle, puzzle."

Missy took the key from Penelope and turned it around in her hands. "The answer is obvious," she said.

"You solved it?" exclaimed Harold.

"No, I mean, we just have to keep looking until we figure out what it opens. Or figure out how it will lead us to something valuable. We've done half the work. We found the key. We can't give up now."

Lester yawned.

"It's bedtime for parrots and pigs," announced Penelope.

"Go on to sleep," said Missy kindly. "It's late."

But Lester shook his head.

"Back to our search?" said Harold as Penelope's eyes began to close.

The search continued. Missy, Lester, and Harold went over every inch of the attic again and were about to start for a third time when Harold cleared his throat. "Didn't someone famous once say that the definition of insanity is doing the same thing over and over and expecting different results?"

"I don't know, but we must be missing something," replied Missy. And that was when she pushed her way through a rack of old winter coats and pirate shirts and, on the wall behind them, felt a doorknob. "Oh!" she exclaimed.

Harold and Lester crowded behind her. "What did you find? What did you find?"

"A doorknob," said Missy. "I didn't know there was a door back here. It's so dark, I can barely see anything."

Helpful Lester clattered all the way downstairs and returned a few minutes later with a flashlight. He aimed it between the clothes.

"Look!" said Harold. "There *is* a door. You can just see the outline."

Missy slowly turned the knob. The door was low and small, and it swung away from them into darkness. Lester crept forward with the flashlight and shined it through the opening.

"What is this little room?" murmured Missy.

"I don't know, but it certainly is a good hiding place," Harold replied. "Just the sort of place a pirate might need in order to safeguard his giant trunk full of gold coins and precious jewels."

"Let's not get ahead of ourselves," said Missy. She felt around for a light switch but couldn't find one. "We'll have to make do with the flashlight."

Lester stepped ahead of them and shone the light around. The room contained exactly one thing. A trunk that was unmistakably a pirate chest.

"I knew it!" cried Harold. He'd been holding the key, and now he handed it to Missy.

Missy stood in front of the trunk. She waited for some sort of sign—for her fingertips to tingle or the key to grow warm. But nothing happened. "Hmm," she said. She inserted the key in the lock.

It wouldn't turn.

"This isn't what the key opens," she said quietly.

"Still, the key led us here," said Harold. "To the trunk, which *must* hold treasure. Don't you understand? The key has done its job."

"I don't think so," Missy replied. "This doesn't feel right."

Harold let out a groan and Lester let out a frustrated oink.

"I'm sorry," said Missy.

"We could still try to open the trunk," said Harold. "I just know something valuable is in there. We could try to open the box and the drawer and even the tool chest, too."

Missy shook her head. "No. Those things don't belong to me. Come on." She led the way out of the secret room and sat down on the carton of books.

"What are you going to do?" asked Harold. "There's no food in your refrigerator, no food for the animals. You're down to your last penny."

"I know. But Auntie has given me a puzzle, and she must think I'm clever enough and perseverant enough to solve it." Missy turned the key over and over in her hands, like a worry stone. She rubbed her fingers across it. "Oh, no."

"What?" asked Harold.

"We chipped the key. We kept trying it in the locks, and we chipped it. Look."

"How can you chip silver?"

"I don't know." Missy flicked the key with her

thumbnail, and a flake of silver landed on her palm. Suddenly she began to laugh. "The key isn't really silver!" she exclaimed. "This is silver paint."

Harold put his head in his hands. "We found the wrong key? Why is that funny?"

Lester let out another oink.

"No, no! This is even better," cried Missy. "Look." She held out the key. "Look what's underneath the paint."

Harold stared. "Gold," he said finally.

Missy nodded. "The silver key is a solid-gold key. It must be worth a fortune."

~~~~~~~

On a warm autumn Thursday, Missy Piggle-Wiggle sat on the swing on her front porch. Lester sat beside her with a cup of coffee. Penelope perched behind her, dozing; Lightfoot dozed in Missy's lap; and Wag dozed at her feet. Missy very much liked the early fall, when the nights were cool but the days were warm, when the leaves were tinged with flaming orange and yellow, and the chrysanthemums bloomed and the bees still buzzed, but lazily. Still, she sometimes felt sad at this time of year. Another school term had begun, so the upside-down house felt big and empty and lonely, at least until three o'clock, when the children would run laughing through the yard and charge onto the porch. Then they would hold out their art projects and tests and essays for Missy to see.

~~~~~~

Missy looked at her watch. Two-thirty. She thought contentedly of her kitchen, which was once again full of food. Out in the barn, the grain bins were full, too. When Missy and Harold had found out how much the gold key was worth, Harold had let out a long whistle. "That should last you forever," he had said.

"I don't know about forever," said Missy, "but for a good long time if I'm careful."

"Got enough for parrot food?" Penelope had wanted to know.

"Plenty."

Harold had asked Missy how she planned to convert the key to money. "Does a bank take care of that sort of thing?"

Missy had shaken her head. "No, but I know just what to do."

Missy had brought the key not to a bank or a jewelry store but to someplace secret and private that the pirates had long ago told Mr. Piggle-Wiggle about, and Mr. Piggle-Wiggle had told Mrs. Piggle-Wiggle about, and Mrs. Piggle-Wiggle had once told Missy about. Missy had packed up her suitcase, the key hidden inside; clapped her cold-weather hat on her head; and taken an overnight journey on a train that ran only when one called upon the conductor. Harold had stayed at the upside-down house and cared for the animals. When Missy returned the next day carrying two very heavy sacks, she had disappeared into the attic for several minutes. Harold hadn't seen the sacks since.

Missy pushed the swing back and forth with her foot. Across town in a classroom in Little Spring Valley Elementary, Houston Forthright sat patiently in his seat, not making a sound even when Beaufort Crumpet accidentally bumped his arm, causing his pencil to skid messily across his worksheet.

In the Dolittles' house, Sunny sat expectantly in the front hallway. She knew that in half an hour, Egmont would burst through the door, clip her leash to her collar, and run into the yard with her. Sunny surrounded herself with two tennis balls, her stuffed hedgehog, and her tug toy, waiting.

Wareford Montpelier also sat in a classroom. He was tan from his trip to the Jersey Shore and was hard at work on a composition about the things he had done that summer. The composition started with the day he had left Missy's house, since everything that had happened before his overnight visit had been hideously boring and could have been included only in a composition titled "What I Didn't Do This Summer."

Back at the upside-down house, every living creature on the porch came to attention all at once. Penelope began marching in place on Missy's shoulder. Lightfoot and Wag awoke and raised their heads. Lester and Missy looked down the lane. Even a spider creeping along a railing stopped his trek and appeared to be listening.

"Mail!" announced Penelope, and, sure enough, the mail truck turned the corner. A few moments later, it drew to a stop at the end of Missy's walk. Lester and Penelope hurried to meet it.

"Good afternoon, Penelope, Lester," said the letter carrier.

Lester nodded politely, but Penelope rudely extended a wing and squawked, "Give it here."

Tunisia McCarter placed a small stack of envelopes on Penelope's wing. "Have a nice day!" she called.

Penelope took the mail in her beak and flew it to Missy, Lester hurrying after her.

Missy sorted through the letters. Then she gasped. "At last! A letter from Auntie."

The animals leaned in close.

"Read it!" cried Penelope.

Missy turned the envelope over. "Huh," she said. "It's already open." She felt around inside. She turned it upside down and shook it out. Empty.

Lester frowned, pointed to his head, and shrugged his shoulders.

"I *suppose* she could have forgotten to include the letter," said Missy, "but that doesn't sound like Auntie."

"Stolen!" shrieked Penelope, and the house rustled its shutters and banged the front door open and closed.

Missy shook her head. "It's a mystery." Then she

looked at her watch again. "Two fifty-nine. Get ready." She shaded her eyes and gazed down the street.

"Incoming!" squawked Penelope.

The children of Little Spring Valley began to arrive at the upside-down house, and Missy tucked the empty envelope into the pocket of her dress.

THANK YOU FOR READING THIS
FEIWEL AND FRIENDS BOOK.

The friends who made

Missy Piggle-Wiggle
and the
Won't-Walk-the-Dog Cure

possible are:

JEAN FEIWEL, Publisher

LIZ SZABLA, Associate Publisher

RICH DEAS, Senior Creative Director

HOLLY WEST, Editor

ALEXEI ESIKOFF, Executive Managing Editor

KIM WAYMER, Senior Production Manager

ANNA ROBERTO, Editor

CHRISTINE BARCELLONA, Editor

EMILY SETTLE, Administrative Assistant

ANNA POON, Editorial Assistant

CAROL LY, Designer

HAYLEY JOZWIAK, Production Editor

———— ➤ ✦ ⬻ ————

Follow us on Facebook or visit us online at mackids.com.
Our books are friends for life.